PART ONE

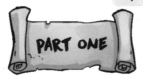

CROSSING THE DESERT

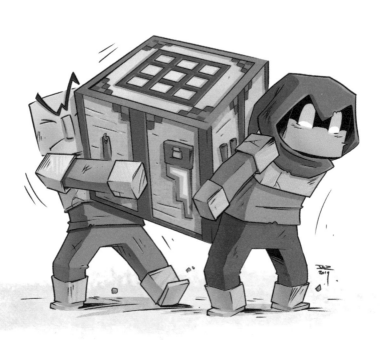

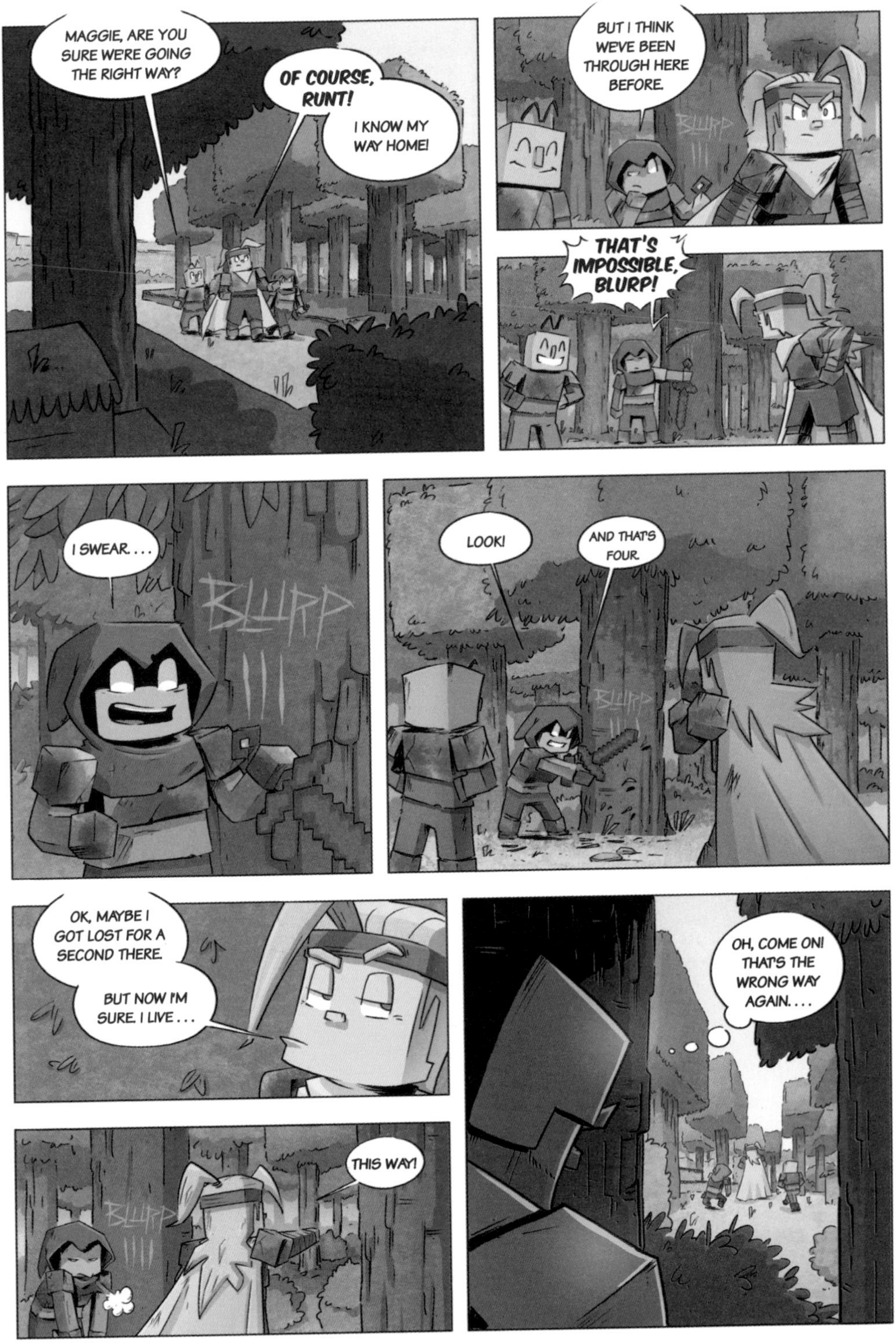
MAGGIE, ARE YOU SURE WE'RE GOING THE RIGHT WAY?
OF COURSE, RUNT!
I KNOW MY WAY HOME!
BUT I THINK WE'VE BEEN THROUGH HERE BEFORE.
BLURP
THAT'S IMPOSSIBLE, BLURP!
I SWEAR. . . .
BLURP
LOOK!
AND THAT'S FOUR.
BLURP
OK, MAYBE I GOT LOST FOR A SECOND THERE.
BUT NOW I'M SURE. I LIVE . . .
OH, COME ON! THAT'S THE WRONG WAY AGAIN. . . .
THIS WAY!
BLURP

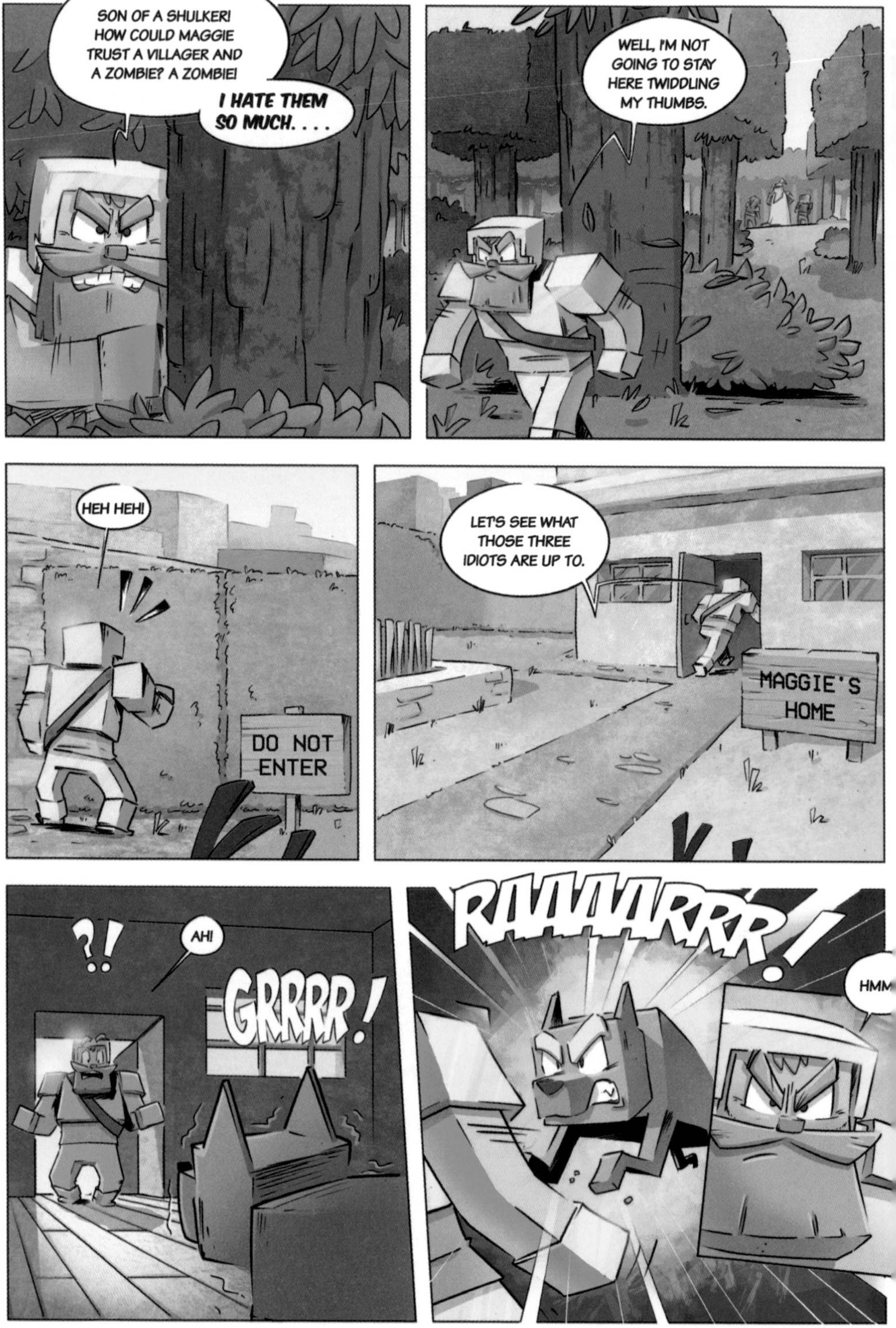
SON OF A SHULKER! HOW COULD MAGGIE TRUST A VILLAGER AND A ZOMBIE? A ZOMBIE!
I HATE THEM SO MUCH. . . .
WELL, I'M NOT GOING TO STAY HERE TWIDDLING MY THUMBS.
HEH HEH!
DO NOT ENTER
LET'S SEE WHAT THOSE THREE IDIOTS ARE UP TO.
MAGGIE'S HOME
?!
AH!
GRRRR!
RAAAARRRR!
HMM

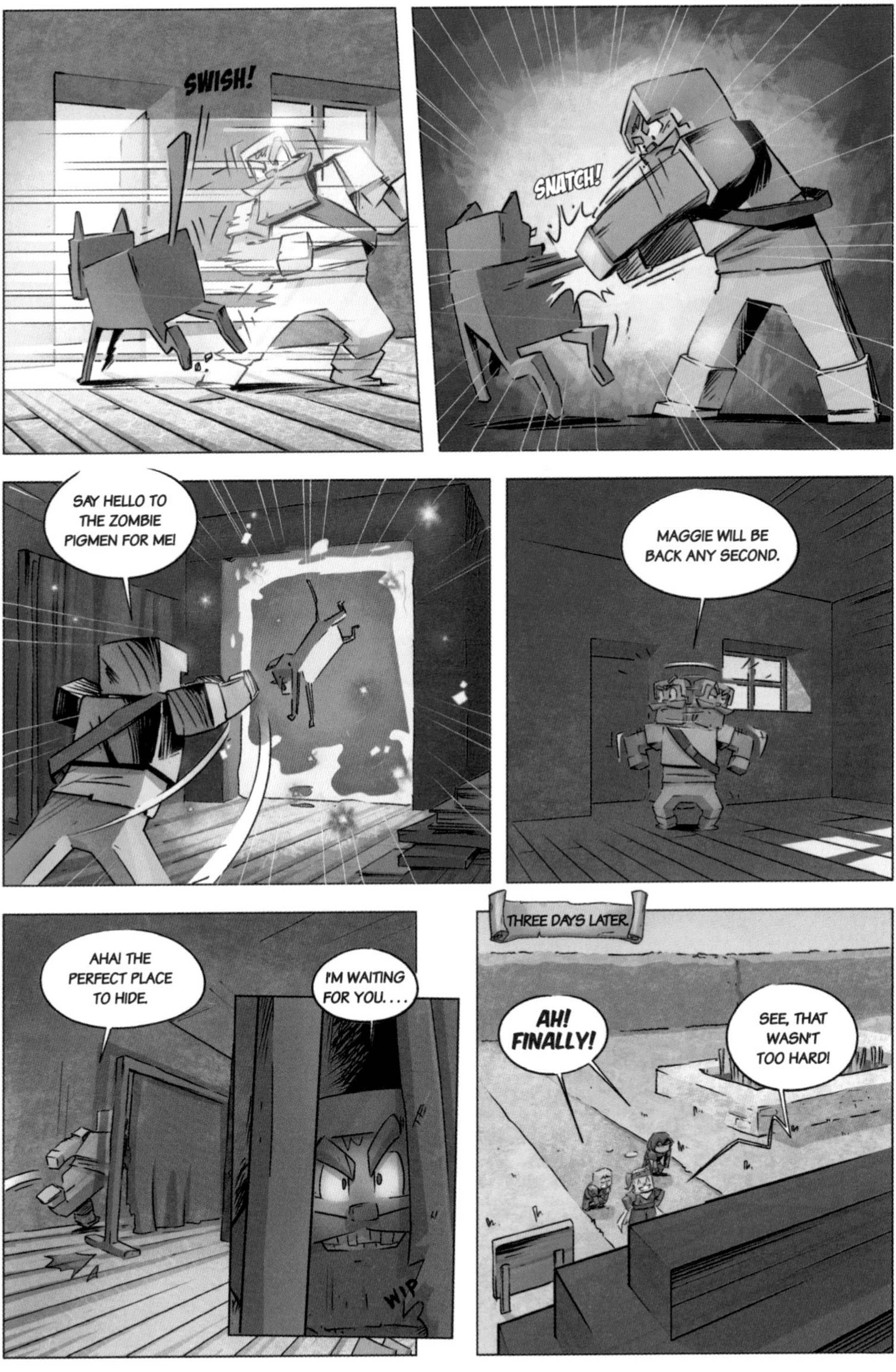
SWISH!
SNATCH!
SAY HELLO TO THE ZOMBIE PIGMEN FOR ME!
MAGGIE WILL BE BACK ANY SECOND.
AHA! THE PERFECT PLACE TO HIDE.
I'M WAITING FOR YOU. . . .
WIP
THREE DAYS LATER.
AH! FINALLY!
SEE, THAT WASN'T TOO HARD!

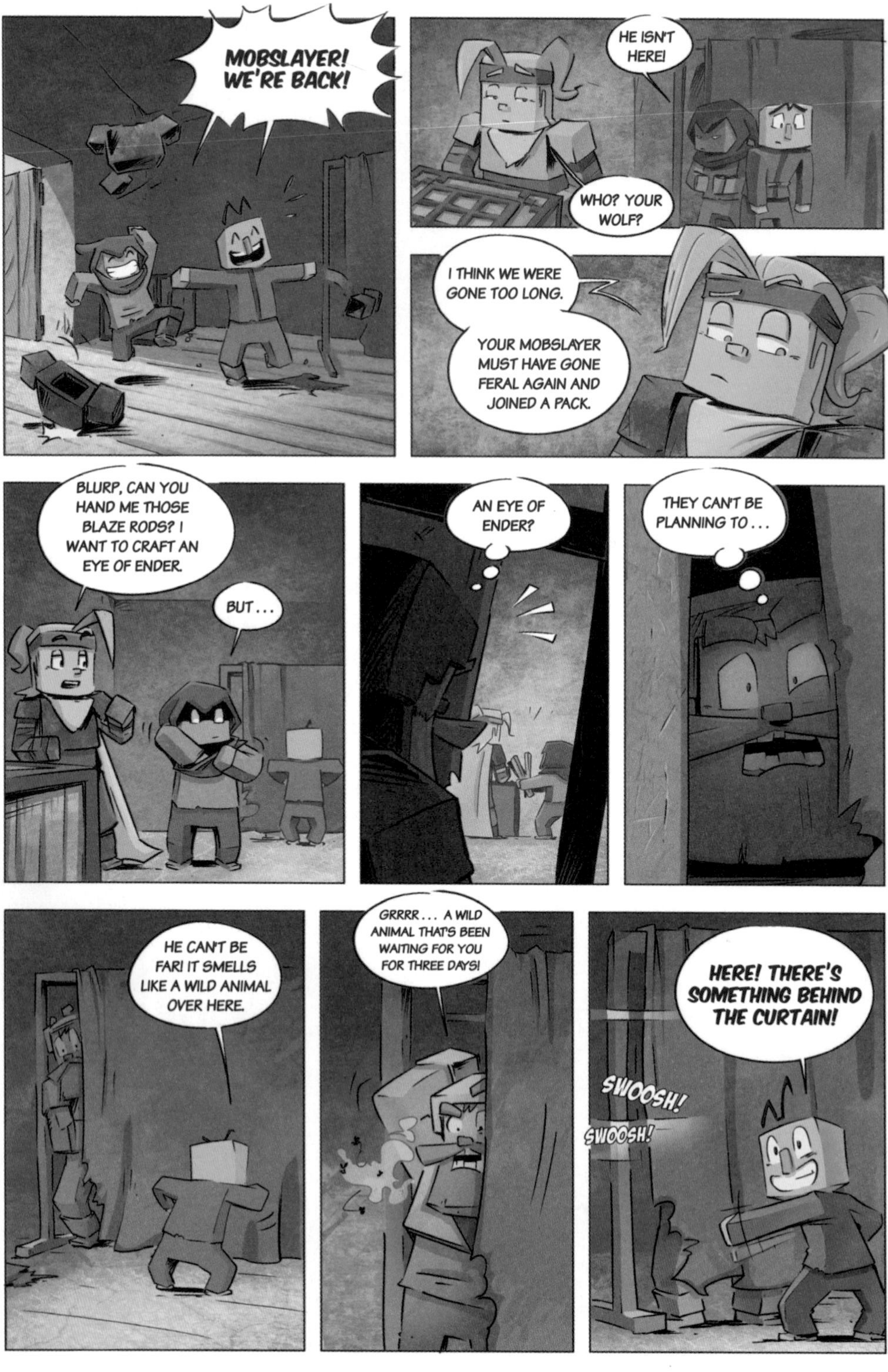
MOBSLAYER! WE'RE BACK!
HE ISN'T HERE!
WHO? YOUR WOLF?
I THINK WE WERE GONE TOO LONG.
YOUR MOBSLAYER MUST HAVE GONE FERAL AGAIN AND JOINED A PACK.
BLURP, CAN YOU HAND ME THOSE BLAZE RODS? I WANT TO CRAFT AN EYE OF ENDER.
BUT . . .
AN EYE OF ENDER?
THEY CAN'T BE PLANNING TO . . .
HE CAN'T BE FAR! IT SMELLS LIKE A WILD ANIMAL OVER HERE.
GRRRR . . . A WILD ANIMAL THAT'S BEEN WAITING FOR YOU FOR THREE DAYS!
HERE! THERE'S SOMETHING BEHIND THE CURTAIN!
SWOOSH!
SWOOSH!

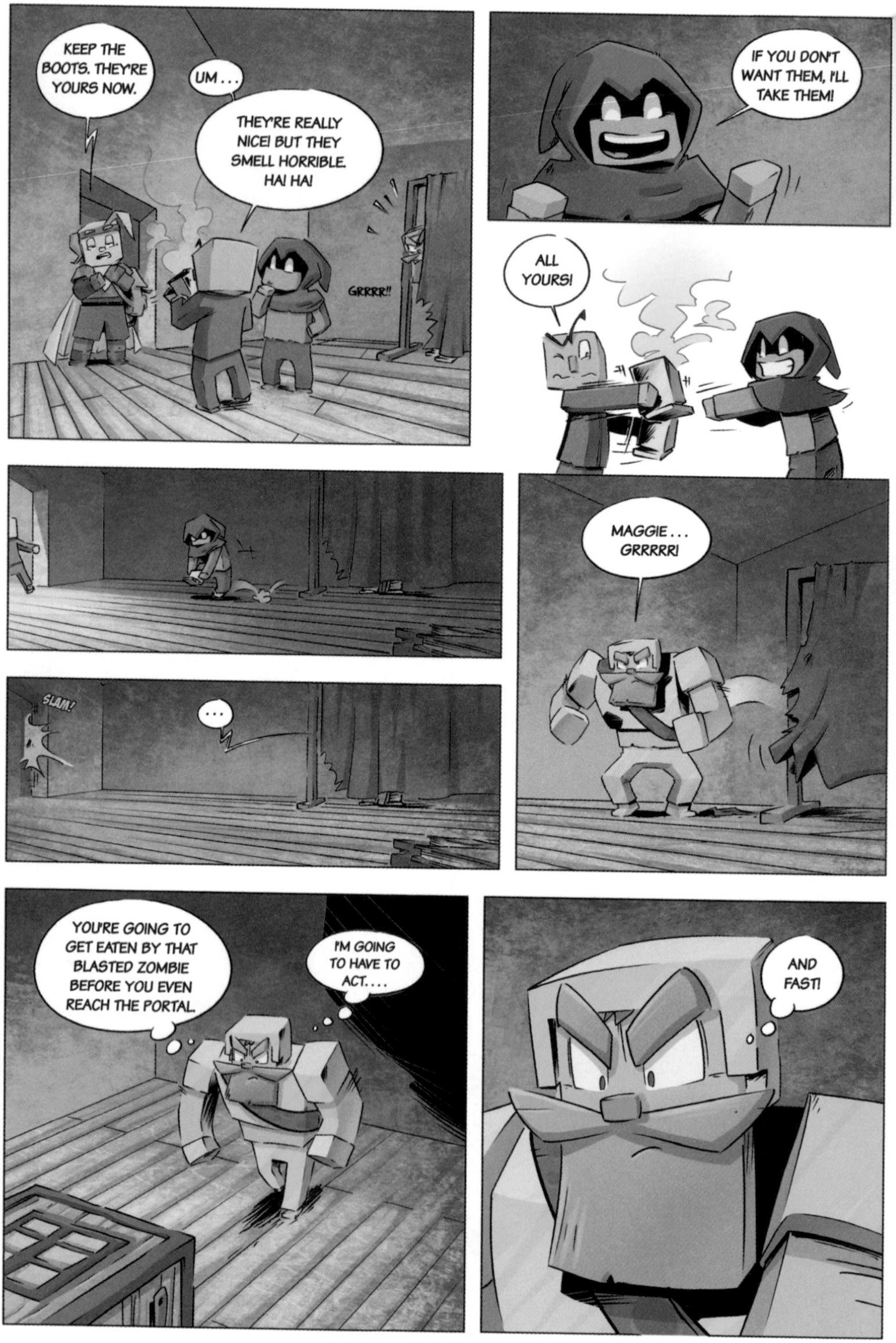
KEEP THE BOOTS. THEY'RE YOURS NOW.
UM . . .
THEY'RE REALLY NICE! BUT THEY SMELL HORRIBLE. HA! HA!
GRRRR!!
IF YOU DON'T WANT THEM, I'LL TAKE THEM!
ALL YOURS!
SLAM!
. . .
MAGGIE . . . GRRRRR!
YOU'RE GOING TO GET EATEN BY THAT BLASTED ZOMBIE BEFORE YOU EVEN REACH THE PORTAL.
I'M GOING TO HAVE TO ACT. . . .
AND FAST!

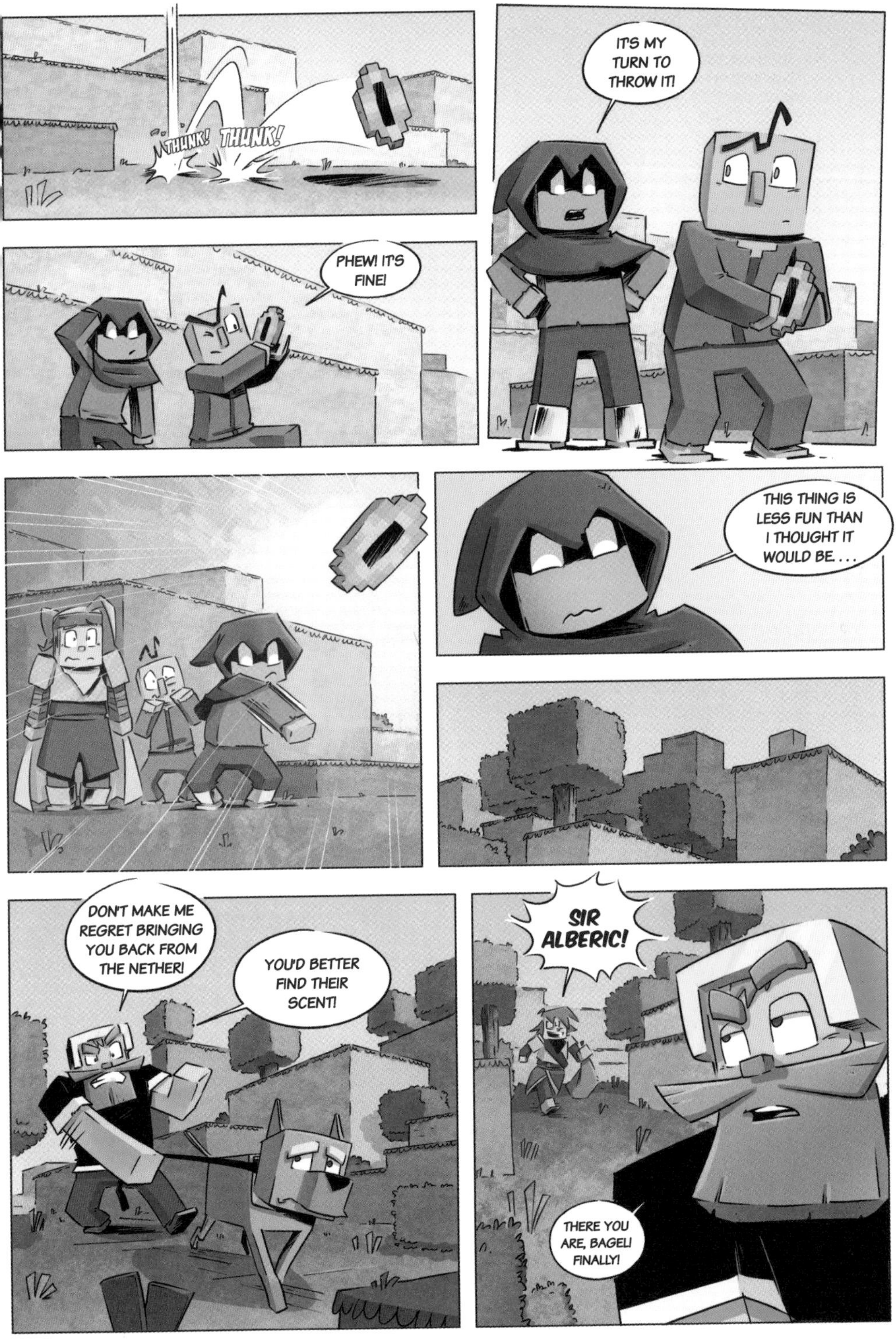
THUNK! THUNK!
IT'S MY TURN TO THROW IT!
PHEW! IT'S FINE!
THIS THING IS LESS FUN THAN I THOUGHT IT WOULD BE. . .
DON'T MAKE ME REGRET BRINGING YOU BACK FROM THE NETHER!
YOU'D BETTER FIND THEIR SCENT!
SIR ALBERIC!
THERE YOU ARE, BAGEL! FINALLY!

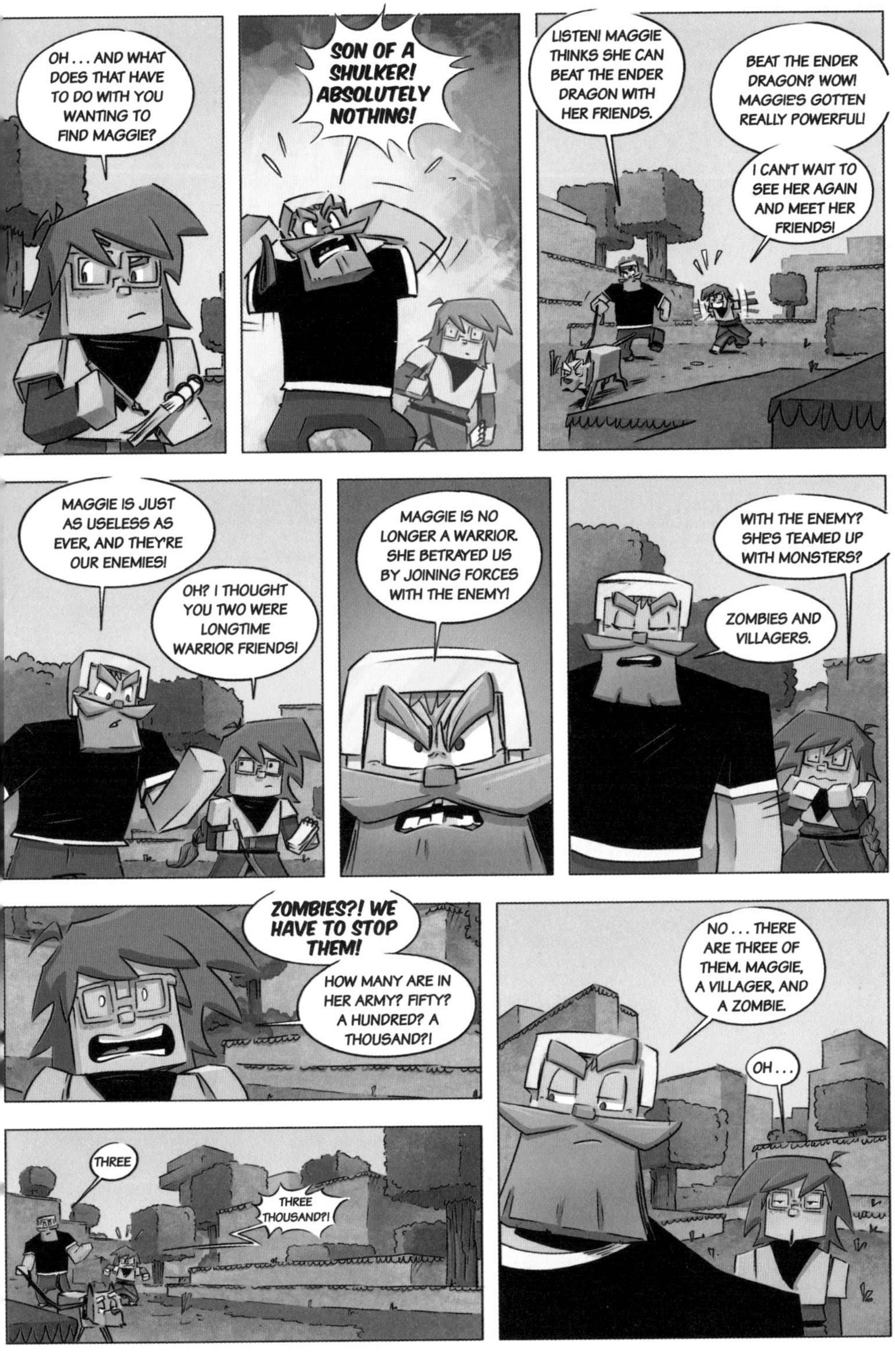
OH . . . AND WHAT DOES THAT HAVE TO DO WITH YOU WANTING TO FIND MAGGIE?
SON OF A SHULKER! ABSOLUTELY NOTHING!
LISTEN! MAGGIE THINKS SHE CAN BEAT THE ENDER DRAGON WITH HER FRIENDS.
BEAT THE ENDER DRAGON? WOW! MAGGIE'S GOTTEN REALLY POWERFUL!
I CAN'T WAIT TO SEE HER AGAIN AND MEET HER FRIENDS!
MAGGIE IS JUST AS USELESS AS EVER, AND THEY'RE OUR ENEMIES!
OH? I THOUGHT YOU TWO WERE LONGTIME WARRIOR FRIENDS!
MAGGIE IS NO LONGER A WARRIOR. SHE BETRAYED US BY JOINING FORCES WITH THE ENEMY!
WITH THE ENEMY? SHE'S TEAMED UP WITH MONSTERS?
ZOMBIES AND VILLAGERS.
ZOMBIES?! WE HAVE TO STOP THEM!
HOW MANY ARE IN HER ARMY? FIFTY? A HUNDRED? A THOUSAND?!
THREE
THREE THOUSAND?!
NO . . . THERE ARE THREE OF THEM. MAGGIE, A VILLAGER, AND A ZOMBIE.
OH . . .

15

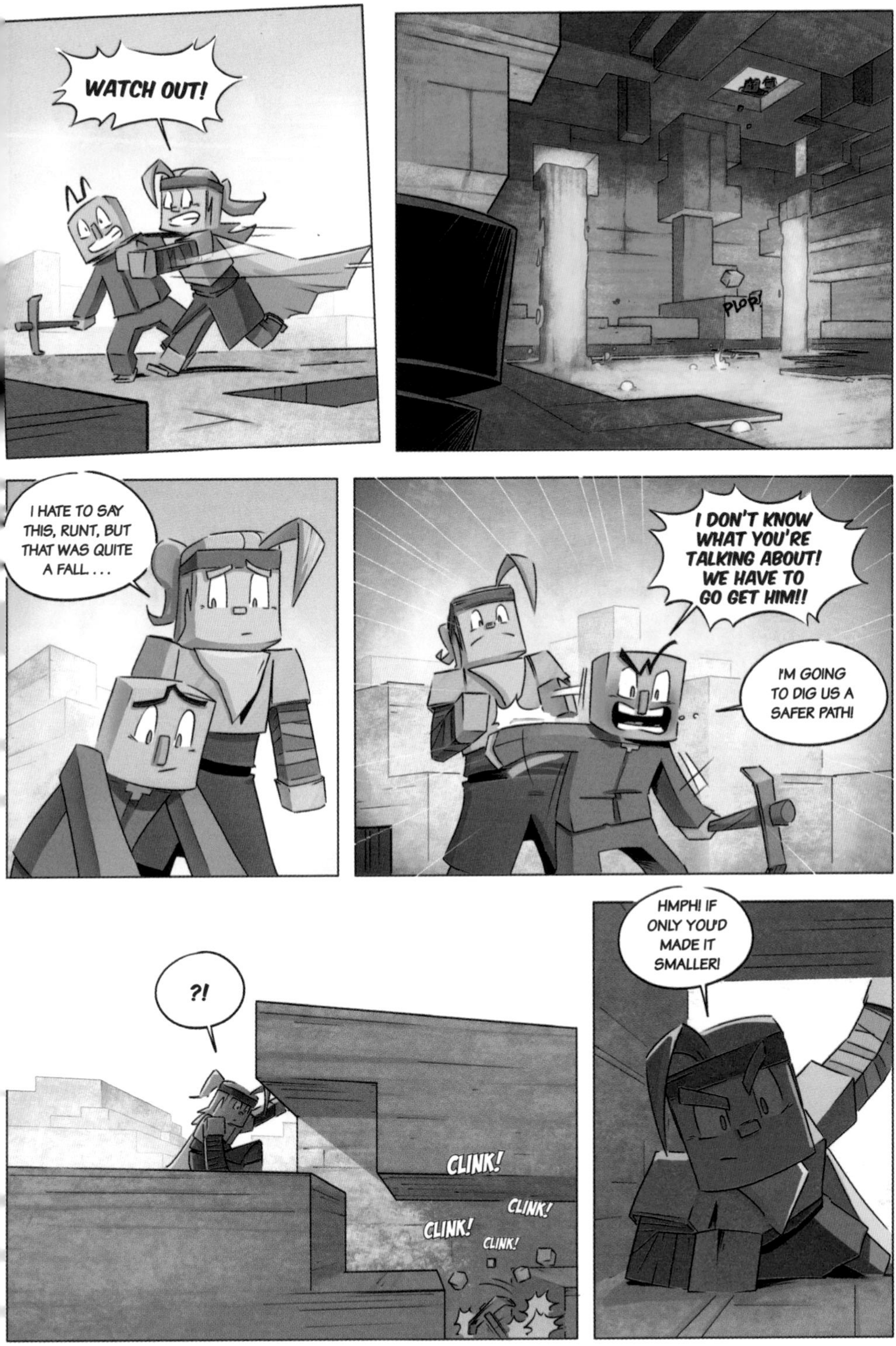

WATCH OUT!
PLOP!
I HATE TO SAY THIS, RUNT, BUT THAT WAS QUITE A FALL . . .
I DON'T KNOW WHAT YOU'RE TALKING ABOUT! WE HAVE TO GO GET HIM!!
I'M GOING TO DIG US A SAFER PATH!
?!
CLINK!
CLINK!
CLINK!
CLINK!
HMPH! IF ONLY YOU'D MADE IT SMALLER!

RUNT?

RUNT, ARE YOU OK?

I THINK SO....

NOW TO FIND BLURP.

RUNT, THERE'S NO POINT.... THERE ARE ONLY MONSTERS HERE.

NO BLURP OVER HERE!

LOOK OUT! A ZOMBIE!

HI!

BLURP! YOU'RE NOT DEAD?!

NO. I MEAN, YES. I'M UNDEAD, SO...

21

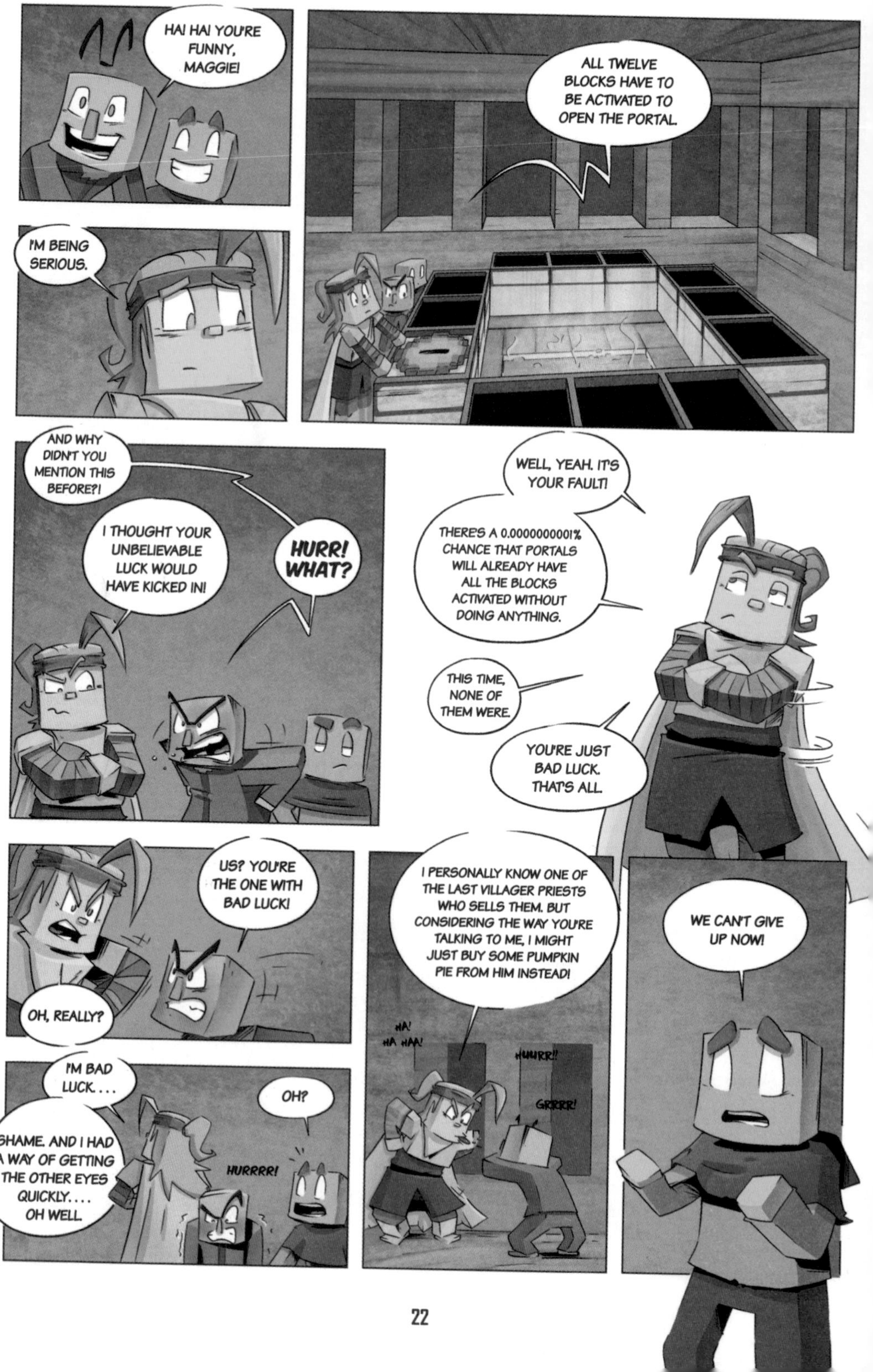
HA! HA! YOU'RE FUNNY, MAGGIE!
I'M BEING SERIOUS.
ALL TWELVE BLOCKS HAVE TO BE ACTIVATED TO OPEN THE PORTAL.
AND WHY DIDN'T YOU MENTION THIS BEFORE?!
I THOUGHT YOUR UNBELIEVABLE LUCK WOULD HAVE KICKED IN!
HURR! WHAT?
WELL, YEAH. IT'S YOUR FAULT!
THERE'S A 0.0000000001% CHANCE THAT PORTALS WILL ALREADY HAVE ALL THE BLOCKS ACTIVATED WITHOUT DOING ANYTHING.
THIS TIME, NONE OF THEM WERE.
YOU'RE JUST BAD LUCK. THAT'S ALL.
US? YOU'RE THE ONE WITH BAD LUCK!
OH, REALLY?
I'M BAD LUCK. . . .
OH?
SHAME. AND I HAD A WAY OF GETTING THE OTHER EYES QUICKLY. . . . OH WELL.
HURRRR!
I PERSONALLY KNOW ONE OF THE LAST VILLAGER PRIESTS WHO SELLS THEM. BUT CONSIDERING THE WAY YOU'RE TALKING TO ME, I MIGHT JUST BUY SOME PUMPKIN PIE FROM HIM INSTEAD!
HA! HA HAA!
HUURR!!
GRRRR!
WE CAN'T GIVE UP NOW!

26

27

29

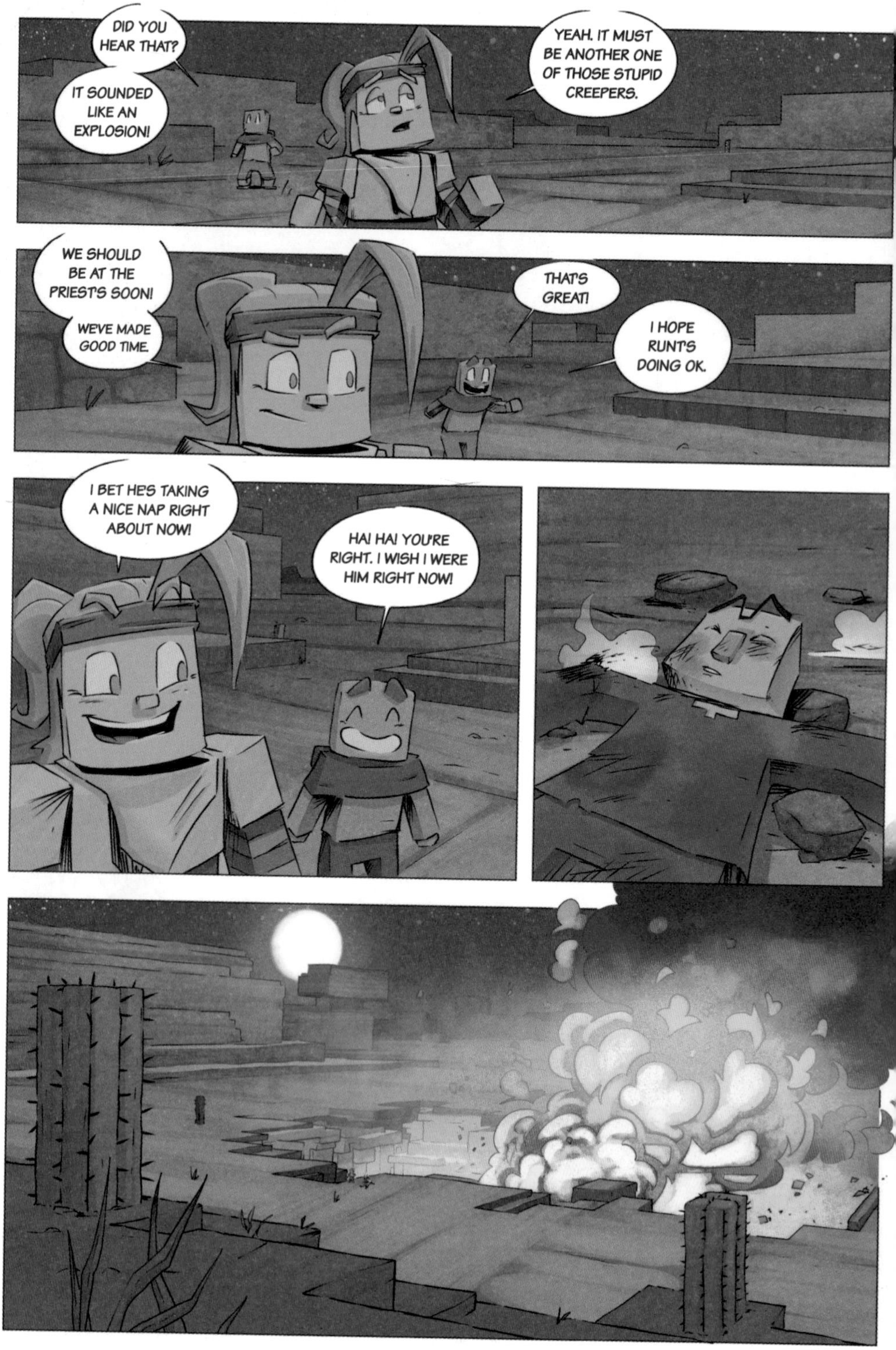
DID YOU HEAR THAT?
IT SOUNDED LIKE AN EXPLOSION!
YEAH. IT MUST BE ANOTHER ONE OF THOSE STUPID CREEPERS.
WE SHOULD BE AT THE PRIEST'S SOON!
WEVE MADE GOOD TIME.
THAT'S GREAT!
I HOPE RUNT'S DOING OK.
I BET HE'S TAKING A NICE NAP RIGHT ABOUT NOW!
HA! HA! YOU'RE RIGHT. I WISH I WERE HIM RIGHT NOW!

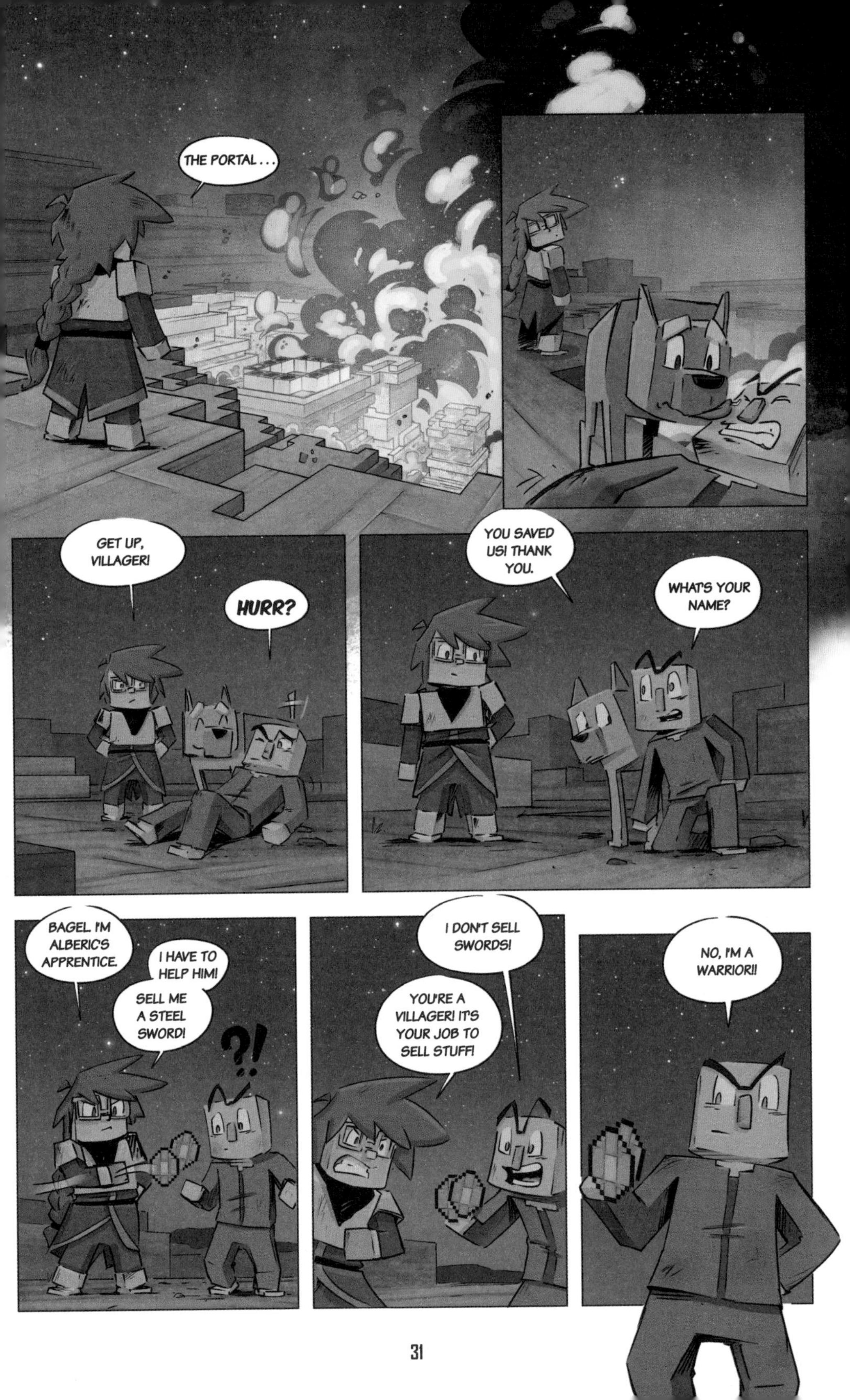
THE PORTAL . . .
GET UP, VILLAGER!
HURR?
YOU SAVED US! THANK YOU.
WHAT'S YOUR NAME?
BAGEL. I'M ALBERIC'S APPRENTICE.
I HAVE TO HELP HIM!
SELL ME A STEEL SWORD!
?!
I DON'T SELL SWORDS!
YOU'RE A VILLAGER! IT'S YOUR JOB TO SELL STUFF!
NO, I'M A WARRIOR!!

BETTER THINGS TO DO?!

YES! AND IT'S NONE OF YOUR BUSINESS.

ANYWAY, BREAK TIME IS OVER.

WE WERE JUST ABOUT TO LEAVE.

THERE'S NO POINT TO GOING TO SEE THE VILLAGER PRIEST!

HE DOESN'T HAVE WHAT YOU'RE LOOKING FOR ANYMORE!

WHAT DO YOU MEAN?!

LIAR. YOU DON'T KNOW ANYTHING!

MASTER MAGGIE, PLEASE HELP ME SAVE SIR ALBERIC! I BEG YOU!

?!

IS HE REALLY IN DANGER?

NO! I DON'T BELIEVE YOU! ALBERIC HAS ALWAYS BEEN ABLE TO TAKE CARE OF HIMSELF.

HAND ME A SWORD. I'M GOING TO HELP HER.

ME TOO!

I TRUST HER, MAGGIE!

AFTER ALL, SHE SAVED MY LIFE AND BROUGHT MOBSLAYER BACK TO US!

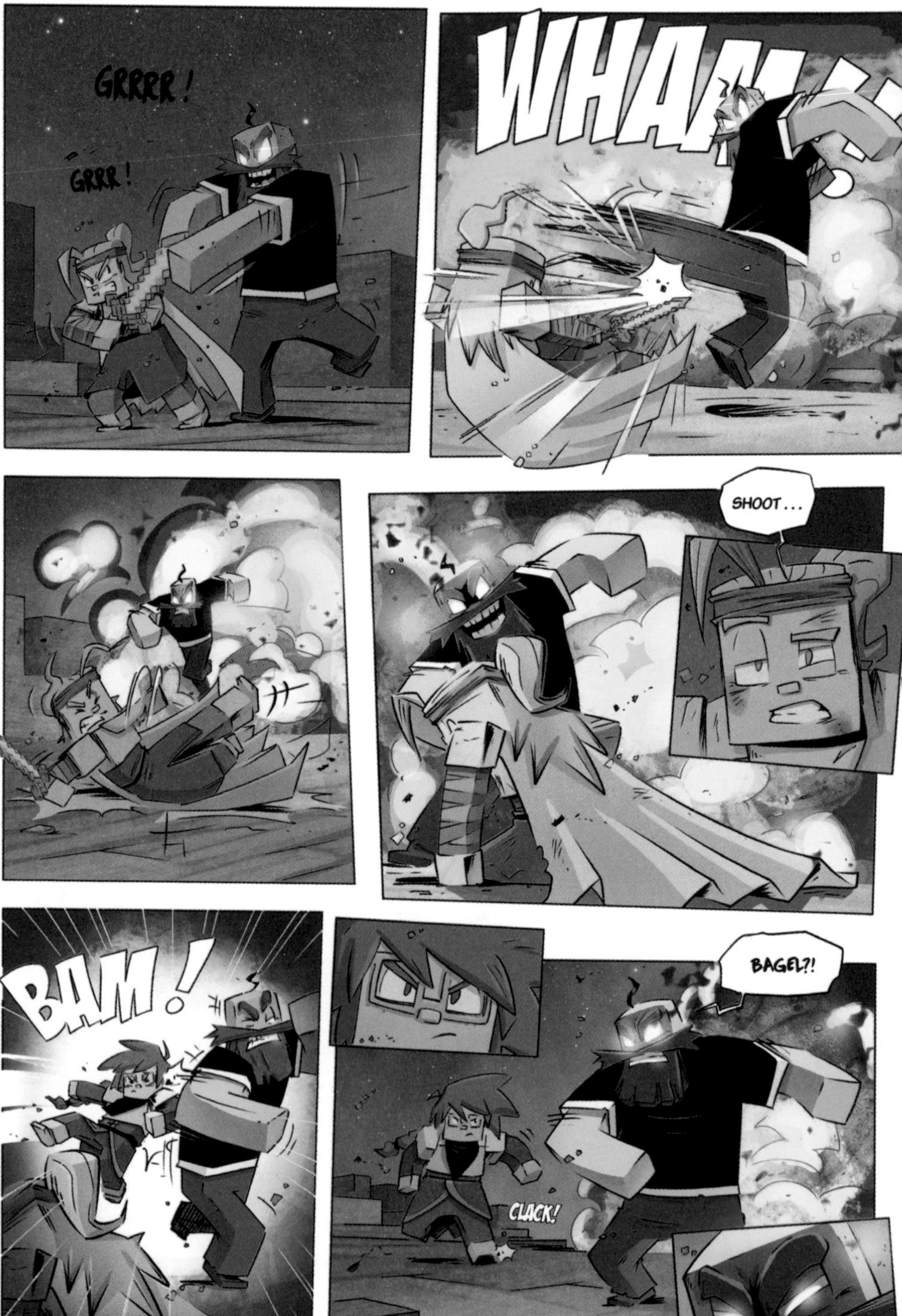
GRRRR!
GRRR!
WHAM
SHOOT...
BAM!
BAGEL?!
CLACK!

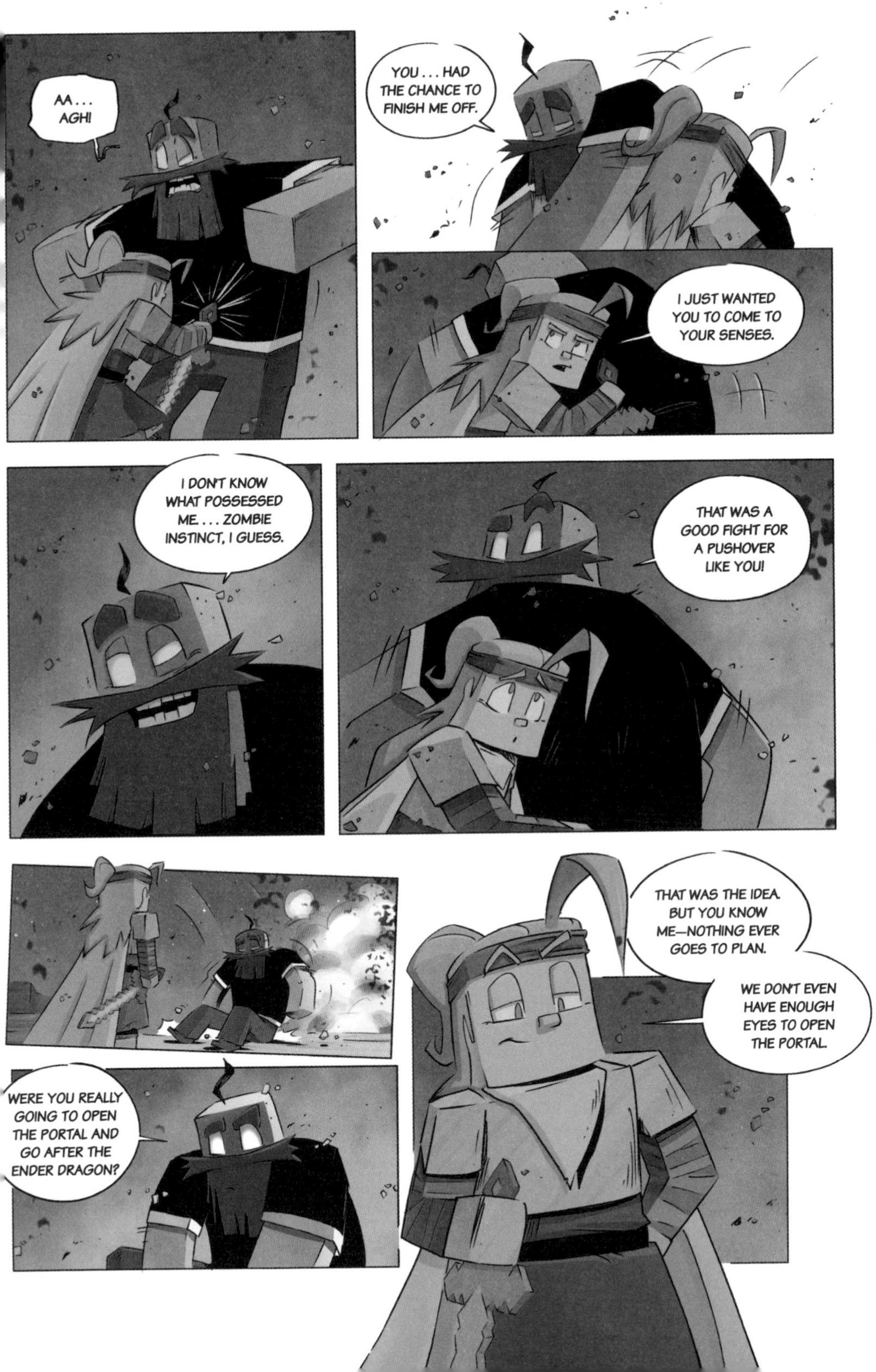
AA . . .
AGH!
YOU . . . HAD THE CHANCE TO FINISH ME OFF.
I JUST WANTED YOU TO COME TO YOUR SENSES.
I DON'T KNOW WHAT POSSESSED ME. . . . ZOMBIE INSTINCT, I GUESS.
THAT WAS A GOOD FIGHT FOR A PUSHOVER LIKE YOU!
WERE YOU REALLY GOING TO OPEN THE PORTAL AND GO AFTER THE ENDER DRAGON?
THAT WAS THE IDEA. BUT YOU KNOW ME—NOTHING EVER GOES TO PLAN.
WE DON'T EVEN HAVE ENOUGH EYES TO OPEN THE PORTAL.

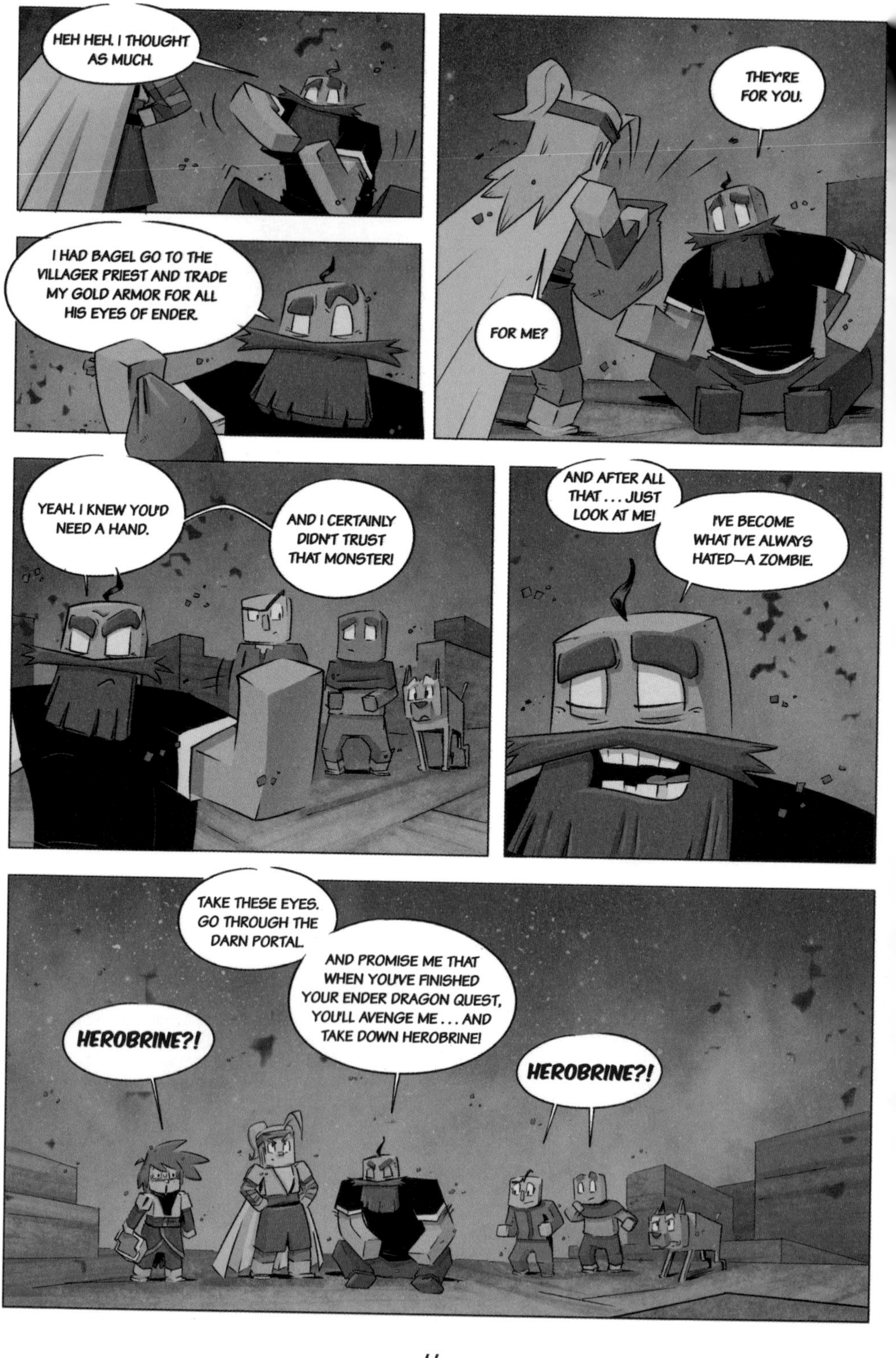
HEH HEH. I THOUGHT AS MUCH.
I HAD BAGEL GO TO THE VILLAGER PRIEST AND TRADE MY GOLD ARMOR FOR ALL HIS EYES OF ENDER.
THEY'RE FOR YOU.
FOR ME?
YEAH. I KNEW YOU'D NEED A HAND.
AND I CERTAINLY DIDN'T TRUST THAT MONSTER!
AND AFTER ALL THAT . . . JUST LOOK AT ME!
I'VE BECOME WHAT I'VE ALWAYS HATED—A ZOMBIE.
TAKE THESE EYES. GO THROUGH THE DARN PORTAL.
AND PROMISE ME THAT WHEN YOU'VE FINISHED YOUR ENDER DRAGON QUEST, YOU'LL AVENGE ME . . . AND TAKE DOWN HEROBRINE!
HEROBRINE?!
HEROBRINE?!

45

PART TWO

WELCOME TO THE END

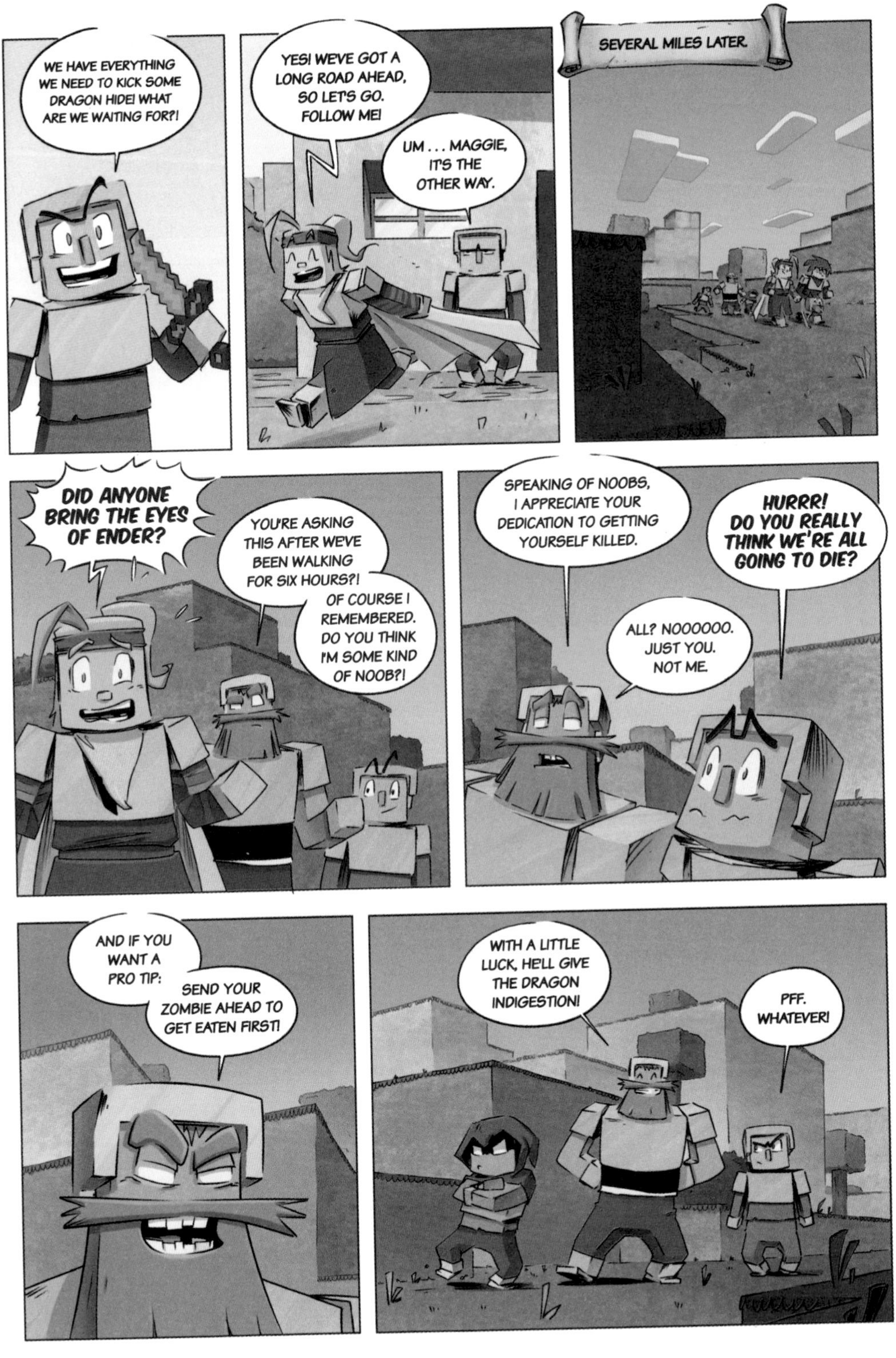
WE HAVE EVERYTHING WE NEED TO KICK SOME DRAGON HIDE! WHAT ARE WE WAITING FOR?!
YES! WE'VE GOT A LONG ROAD AHEAD, SO LET'S GO. FOLLOW ME!
UM . . . MAGGIE, IT'S THE OTHER WAY.
SEVERAL MILES LATER.
DID ANYONE BRING THE EYES OF ENDER?
YOU'RE ASKING THIS AFTER WE'VE BEEN WALKING FOR SIX HOURS?!
OF COURSE I REMEMBERED. DO YOU THINK I'M SOME KIND OF NOOB?!
SPEAKING OF NOOBS, I APPRECIATE YOUR DEDICATION TO GETTING YOURSELF KILLED.
HURRR! DO YOU REALLY THINK WE'RE ALL GOING TO DIE?
ALL? NOOOOOO. JUST YOU. NOT ME.
AND IF YOU WANT A PRO TIP:
SEND YOUR ZOMBIE AHEAD TO GET EATEN FIRST!
WITH A LITTLE LUCK, HE'LL GIVE THE DRAGON INDIGESTION!
PFF. WHATEVER!

RUNT?

AREN'T YOU SCARED?

THAT WE DON'T HAVE ENOUGH APPLES?

NO, SILLY! THAT WE WON'T DEFEAT THE ENDER DRAGON!

WE CAN'T LOSE IF WE ALL WORK TOGETHER!

I'VE HEARD SO MANY SCARY STORIES ABOUT THAT DRAGON. . . .

EVEN THOUGH SIR ALBERIC HAS TRAINED ME WELL,

I'M WORRIED I WON'T BE STRONG ENOUGH.

BLURP AND I HAVE ALREADY BEATEN AN ENDERMAN, PLUS A BLAZE IN THE NETHER!

HEH HEH. THANKS, RUNT!

WE'LL PROTECT YOU!

AND WORST CASE, WE CAN USE OUR SIGNATURE TACTIC!

WHAT'S THAT?

RUNNING AWAY!

WISE GUY! YOU'VE GOT AN ANSWER FOR EVERYTHING.

NOW THE DRAGON'S REPUTATION MAKES MORE SENSE.

IT'S WELL EARNED.

JUST LIKE YOU "EARNED" MY GOLD BOOTS!

HA! HA! HA! HA! HA! HA! HA!

YOU SURE KNOW SOMETHING ABOUT EARNING THINGS.

DON'T BE MAD, BLURP!

I'M GOING TO BED.

YOU'VE GOT TO STOP PICKING ON HIM. BLURP IS A NICE ZOMBIE!

A NICE ZOMBIE?

I'VE NEVER HEARD YOU SAY SOMETHING SO RIDICULOUS!

YOU OUGHT TO KNOW! JUST LOOK IN THE MIRROR!

IT'S NEVER TOO LATE TO CHANGE.

I ONLY CHANGED COLOR!

AFTER WHAT HAPPENED TO US A FEW YEARS BACK,

I COULD NEVER BE ONE OF THEM.

WHAT HAPPENED?

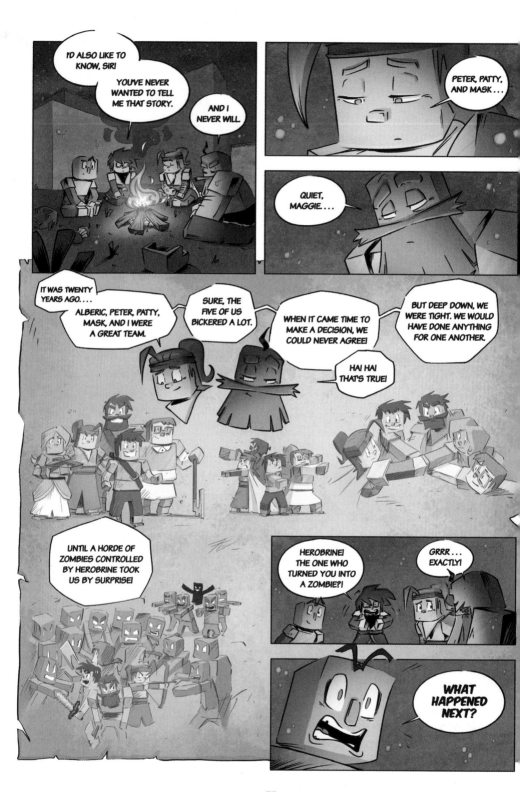

56

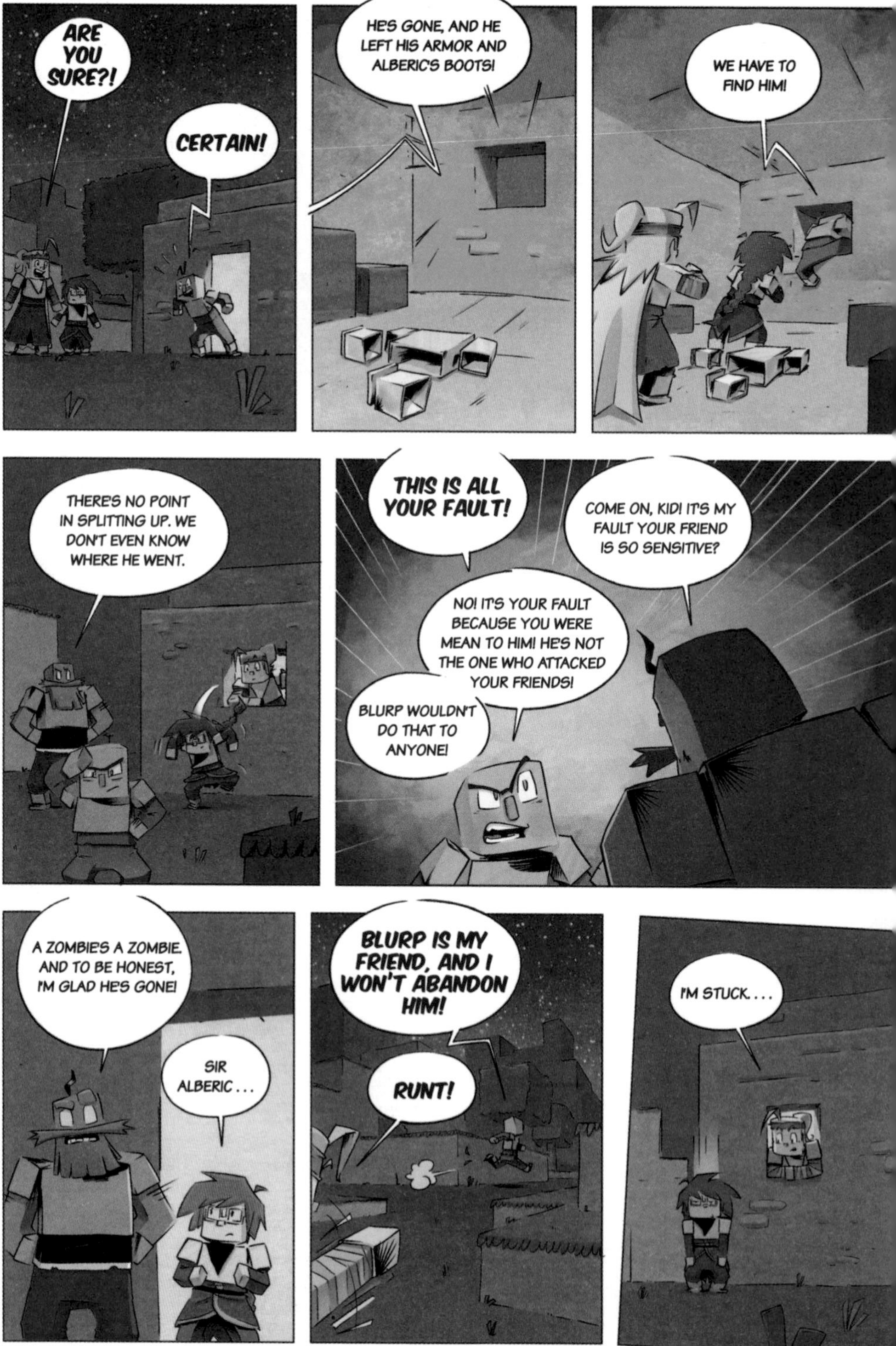
ARE YOU SURE?!
CERTAIN!
HE'S GONE, AND HE LEFT HIS ARMOR AND ALBERIC'S BOOTS!
WE HAVE TO FIND HIM!
THERE'S NO POINT IN SPLITTING UP. WE DON'T EVEN KNOW WHERE HE WENT.
THIS IS ALL YOUR FAULT!
COME ON, KID! IT'S MY FAULT YOUR FRIEND IS SO SENSITIVE?
NO! IT'S YOUR FAULT BECAUSE YOU WERE MEAN TO HIM! HE'S NOT THE ONE WHO ATTACKED YOUR FRIENDS!
BLURP WOULDN'T DO THAT TO ANYONE!
A ZOMBIE'S A ZOMBIE. AND TO BE HONEST, I'M GLAD HE'S GONE!
SIR ALBERIC . . .
BLURP IS MY FRIEND, AND I WON'T ABANDON HIM!
RUNT!
I'M STUCK. . . .

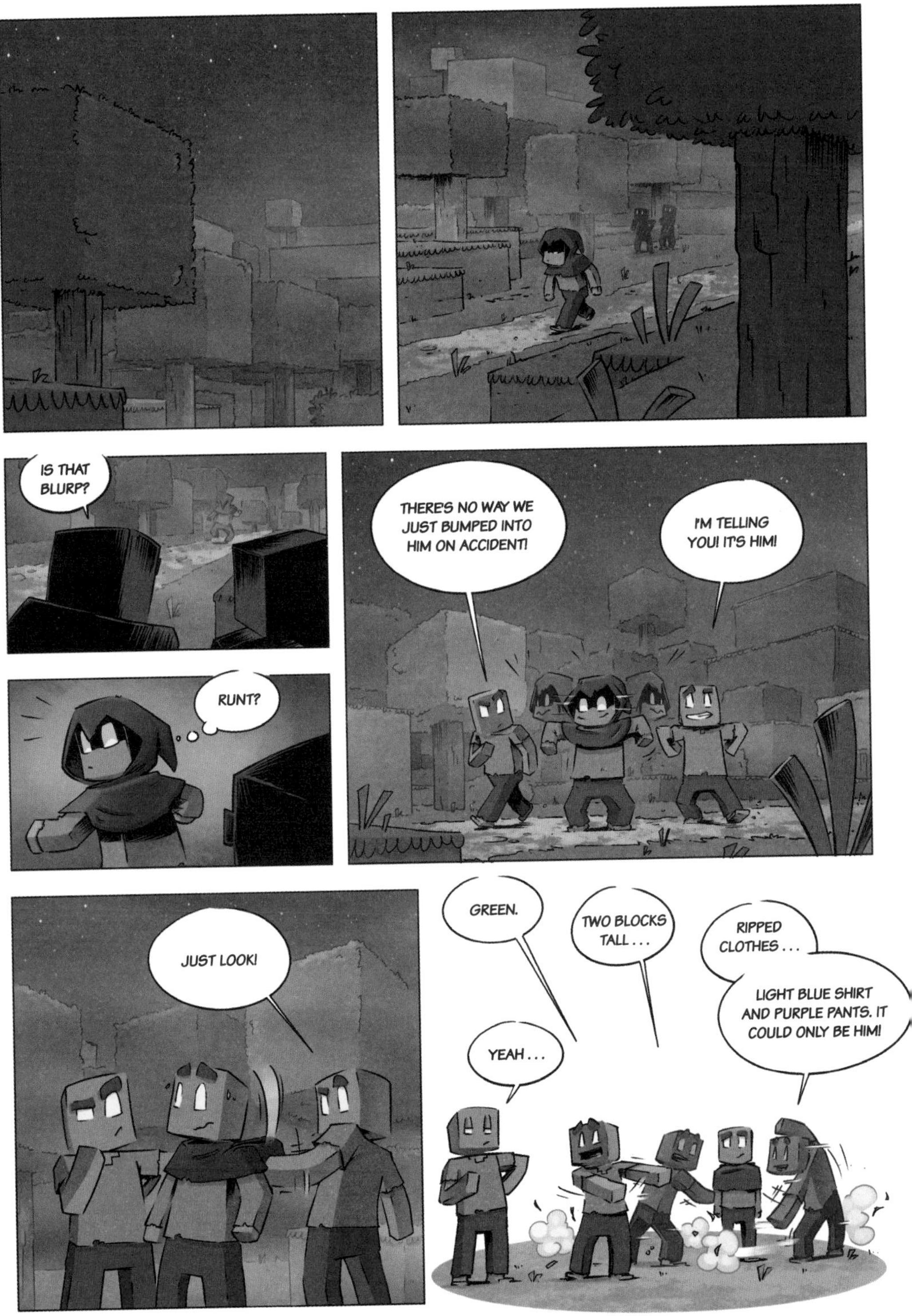
IS THAT BLURP?
RUNT?
THERE'S NO WAY WE JUST BUMPED INTO HIM ON ACCIDENT!
I'M TELLING YOU! IT'S HIM!
JUST LOOK!
GREEN.
TWO BLOCKS TALL . . .
RIPPED CLOTHES . . .
LIGHT BLUE SHIRT AND PURPLE PANTS. IT COULD ONLY BE HIM!
YEAH . . .

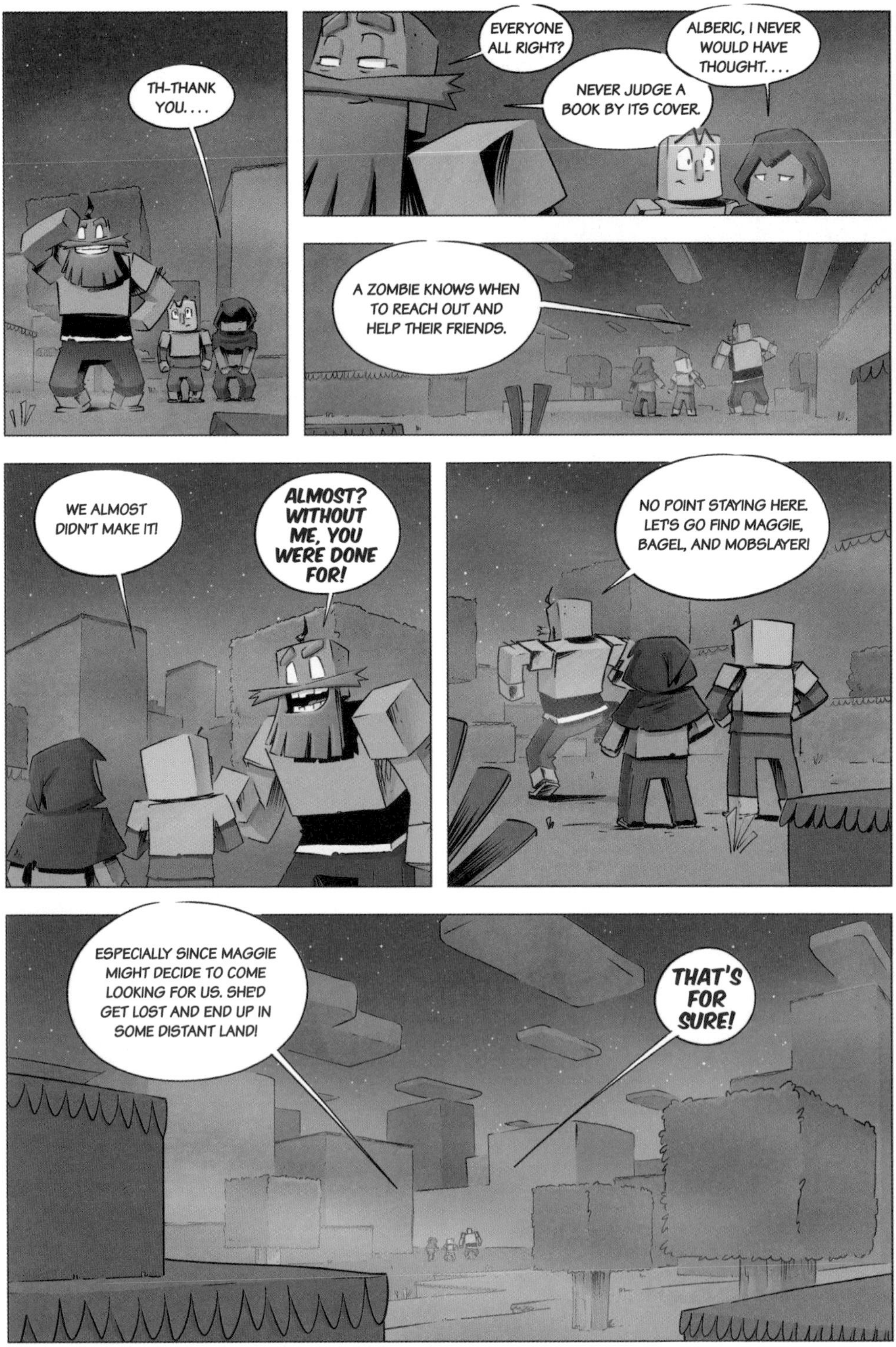
TH-THANK YOU. . . .
EVERYONE ALL RIGHT?
ALBERIC, I NEVER WOULD HAVE THOUGHT. . . .
NEVER JUDGE A BOOK BY ITS COVER.
A ZOMBIE KNOWS WHEN TO REACH OUT AND HELP THEIR FRIENDS.
WE ALMOST DIDN'T MAKE IT!
ALMOST? WITHOUT ME, YOU WERE DONE FOR!
NO POINT STAYING HERE. LET'S GO FIND MAGGIE, BAGEL, AND MOBSLAYER!
ESPECIALLY SINCE MAGGIE MIGHT DECIDE TO COME LOOKING FOR US. SHE'D GET LOST AND END UP IN SOME DISTANT LAND!
THAT'S FOR SURE!

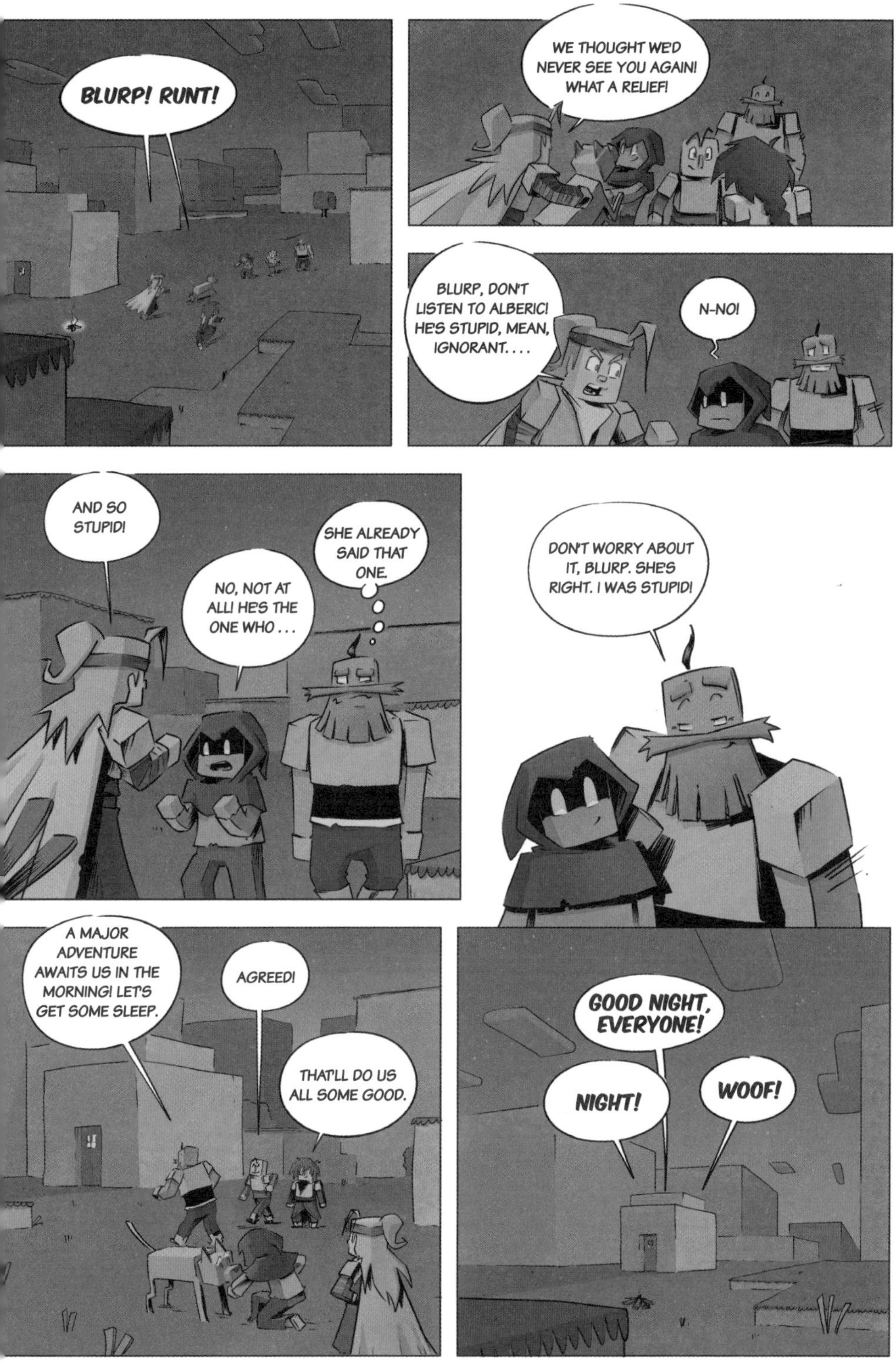
BLURP! RUNT!
WE THOUGHT WE'D NEVER SEE YOU AGAIN! WHAT A RELIEF!
BLURP, DON'T LISTEN TO ALBERIC! HE'S STUPID, MEAN, IGNORANT. . . .
N-NO!
AND SO STUPID!
NO, NOT AT ALL! HE'S THE ONE WHO . . .
SHE ALREADY SAID THAT ONE.
DON'T WORRY ABOUT IT, BLURP. SHE'S RIGHT. I WAS STUPID!
A MAJOR ADVENTURE AWAITS US IN THE MORNING! LET'S GET SOME SLEEP.
AGREED!
THAT'LL DO US ALL SOME GOOD.
GOOD NIGHT, EVERYONE!
NIGHT!
WOOF!

HURR! WAKE UP!

BLURP'S GONE AGAIN!

HMM?

SON OF A SHULKER! AGAIN?!

BLURP!

WHAT'S WRONG? YOU DON'T LIKE FISH?

HAI HAI NO, I LOVE FISH! BUT DON'T BOTHER COOKING MINE. I'M CRAVING RAW FLESH!

THANKS, BLURP!

SEE, ZOMBIES AREN'T SO BAD!

MMMM! THIS IS SO GOOD!

WE NEED OUR STRENGTH TO GO UP AGAINST THE DRAGON!

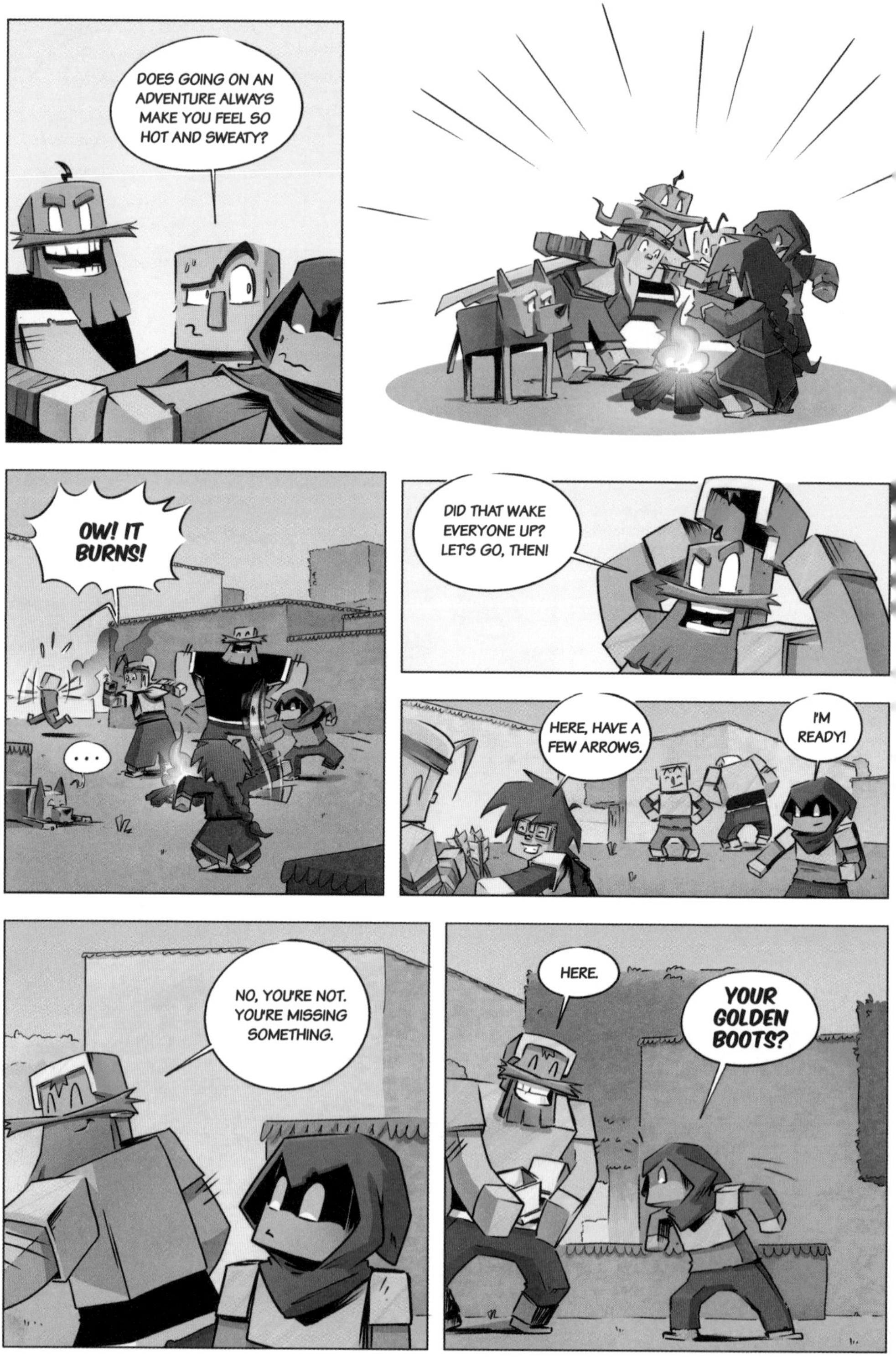

DOES GOING ON AN ADVENTURE ALWAYS MAKE YOU FEEL SO HOT AND SWEATY?
OW! IT BURNS!
...
DID THAT WAKE EVERYONE UP? LET'S GO, THEN!
HERE, HAVE A FEW ARROWS.
I'M READY!
NO, YOU'RE NOT. YOU'RE MISSING SOMETHING.
HERE.
YOUR GOLDEN BOOTS?

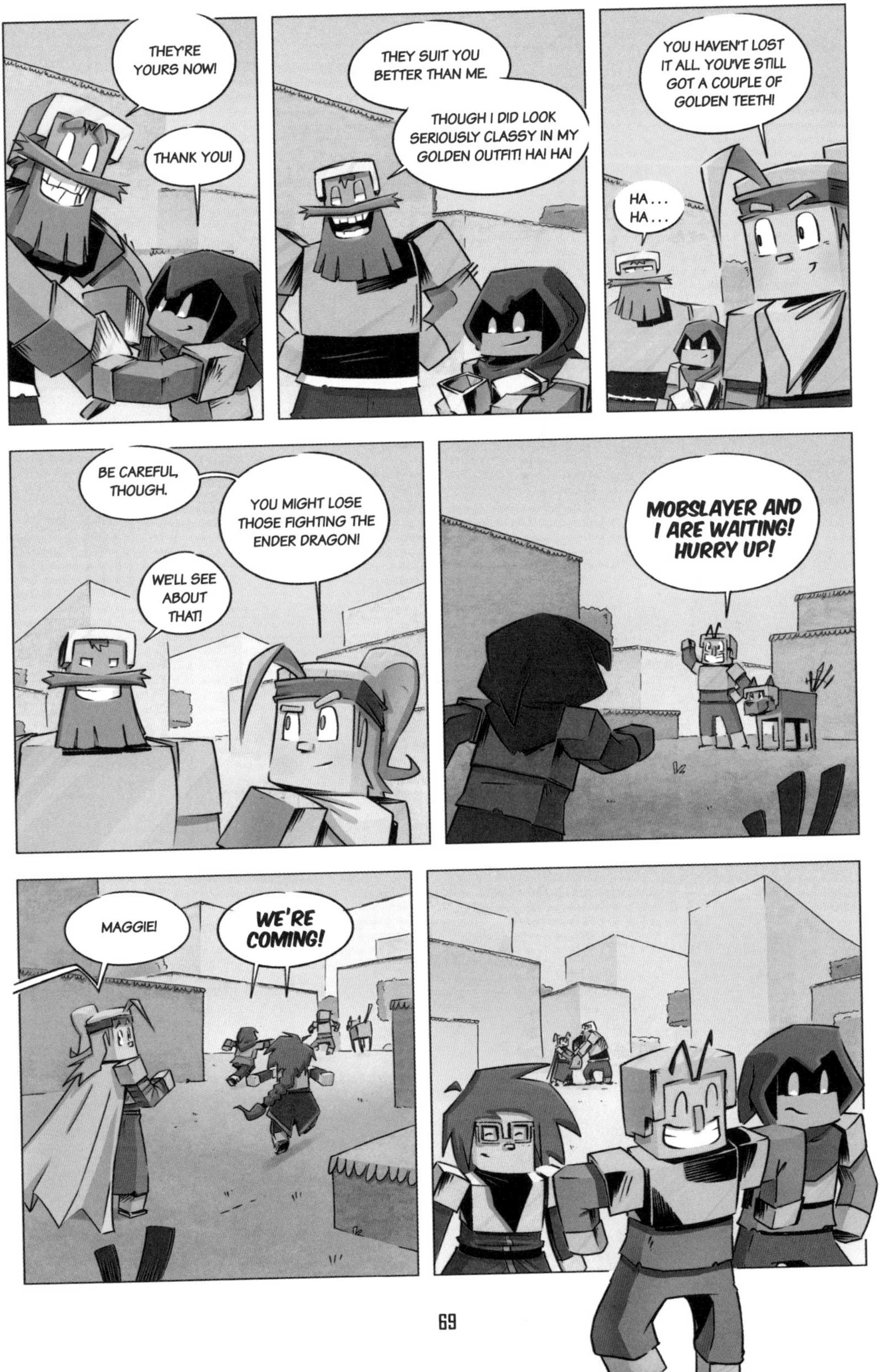
THEY'RE YOURS NOW!
THANK YOU!
THEY SUIT YOU BETTER THAN ME.
THOUGH I DID LOOK SERIOUSLY CLASSY IN MY GOLDEN OUTFIT! HA! HA!
YOU HAVEN'T LOST IT ALL. YOU'VE STILL GOT A COUPLE OF GOLDEN TEETH!
HA . . . HA . . .
BE CAREFUL, THOUGH.
YOU MIGHT LOSE THOSE FIGHTING THE ENDER DRAGON!
WE'LL SEE ABOUT THAT!
MOBSLAYER AND I ARE WAITING! HURRY UP!
MAGGIE!
WE'RE COMING!

70

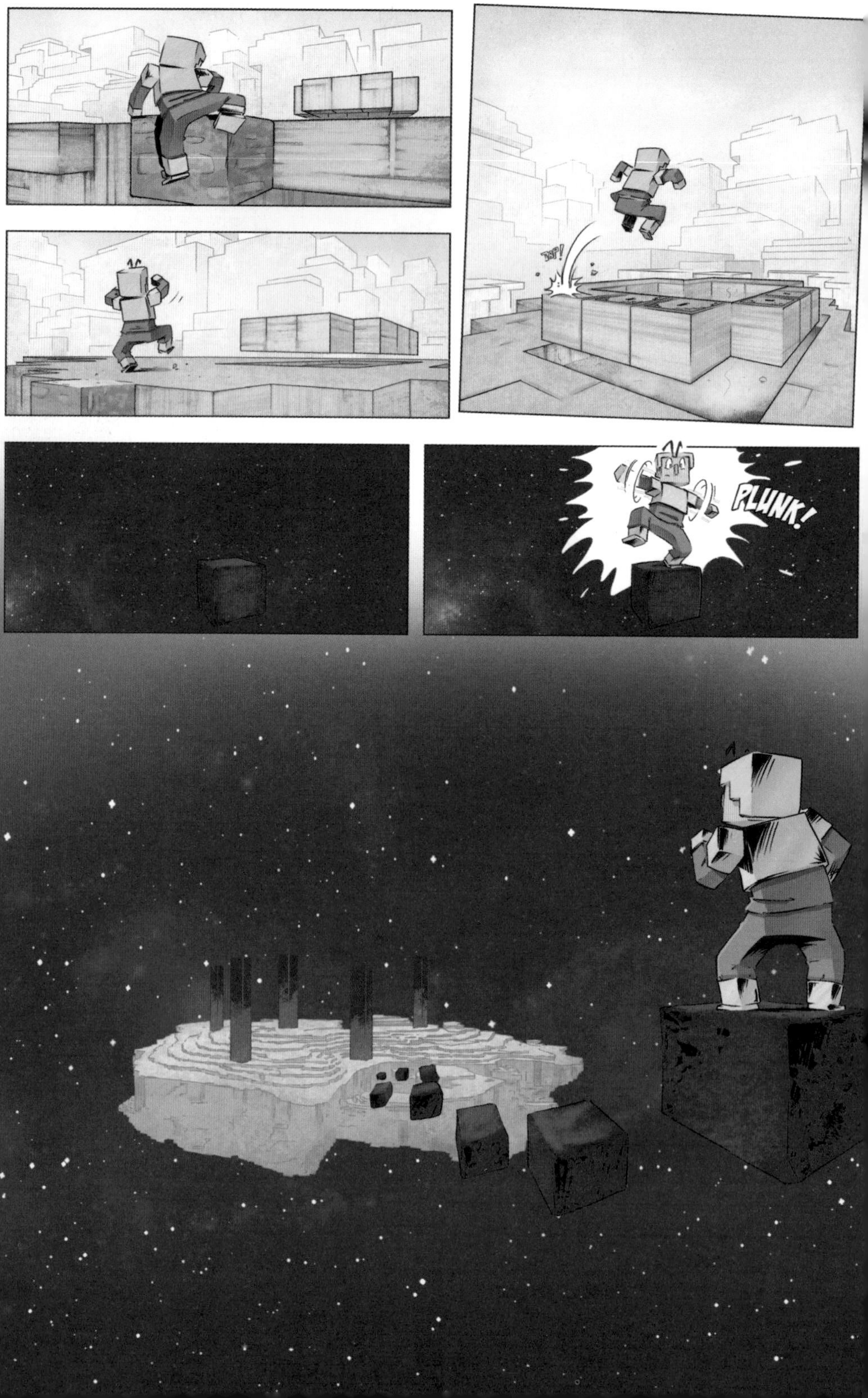
PLUNK!

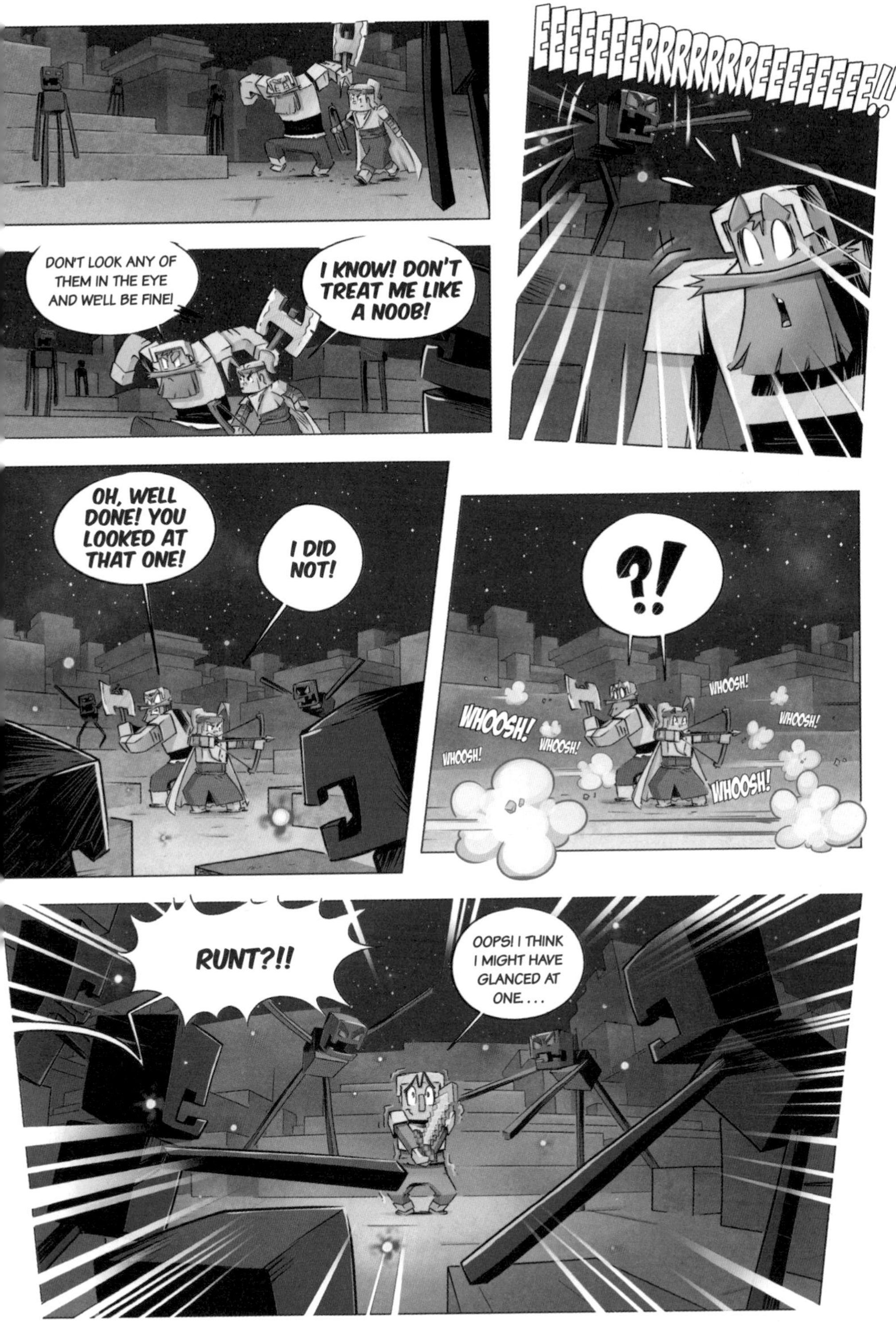

DON'T LOOK ANY OF THEM IN THE EYE AND WE'LL BE FINE!
I KNOW! DON'T TREAT ME LIKE A NOOB!
EEEEEEERRRRRREEEEEEEE!!!
OH, WELL DONE! YOU LOOKED AT THAT ONE!
I DID NOT!
?!
WHOOSH!
WHOOSH!
WHOOSH!
WHOOSH!
WHOOSH!
WHOOSH!
RUNT?!!
OOPS! I THINK I MIGHT HAVE GLANCED AT ONE. . .

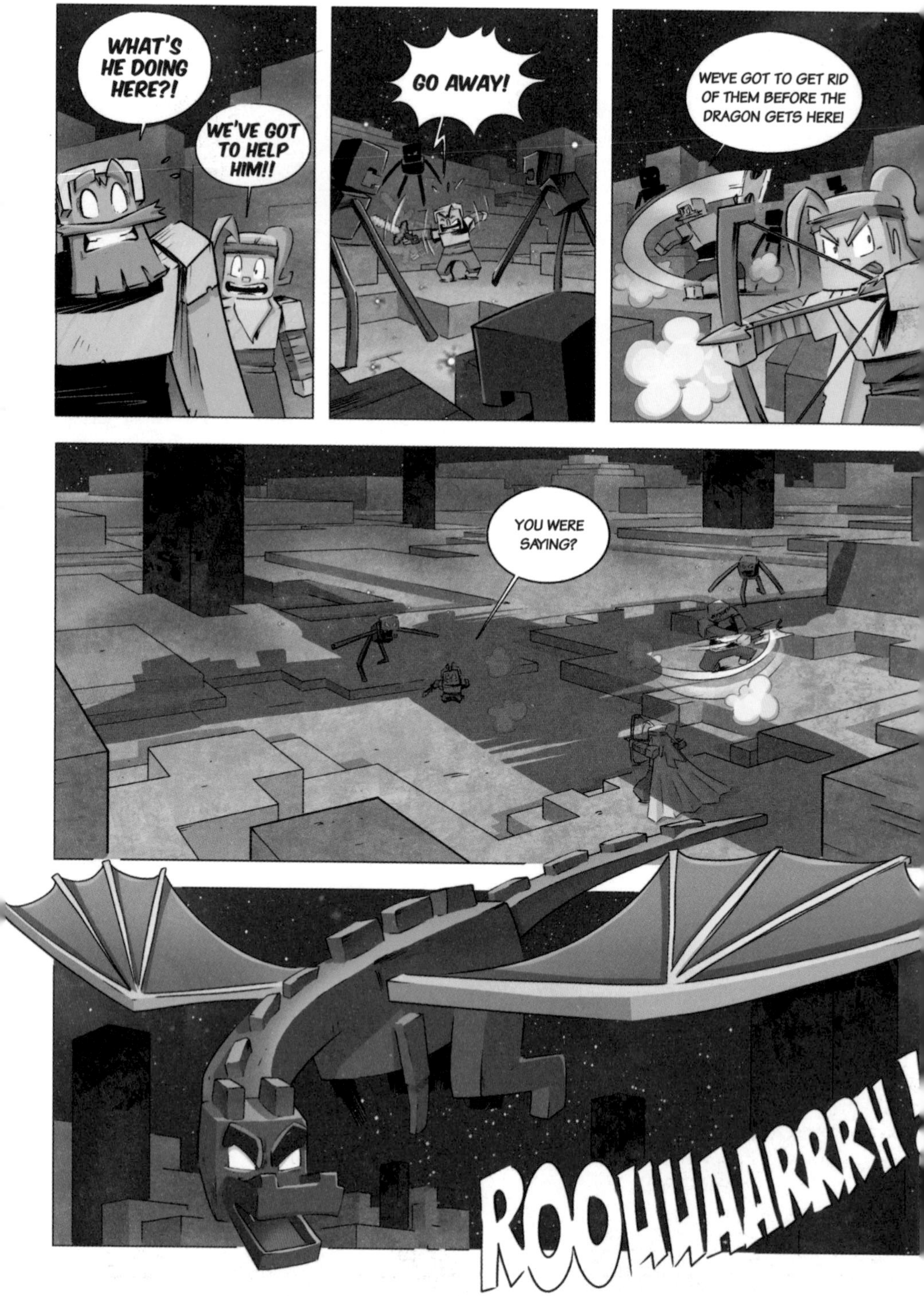
WHAT'S HE DOING HERE?!
WE'VE GOT TO HELP HIM!!
GO AWAY!
WE'VE GOT TO GET RID OF THEM BEFORE THE DRAGON GETS HERE!
YOU WERE SAYING?
ROOHHAARRRH!

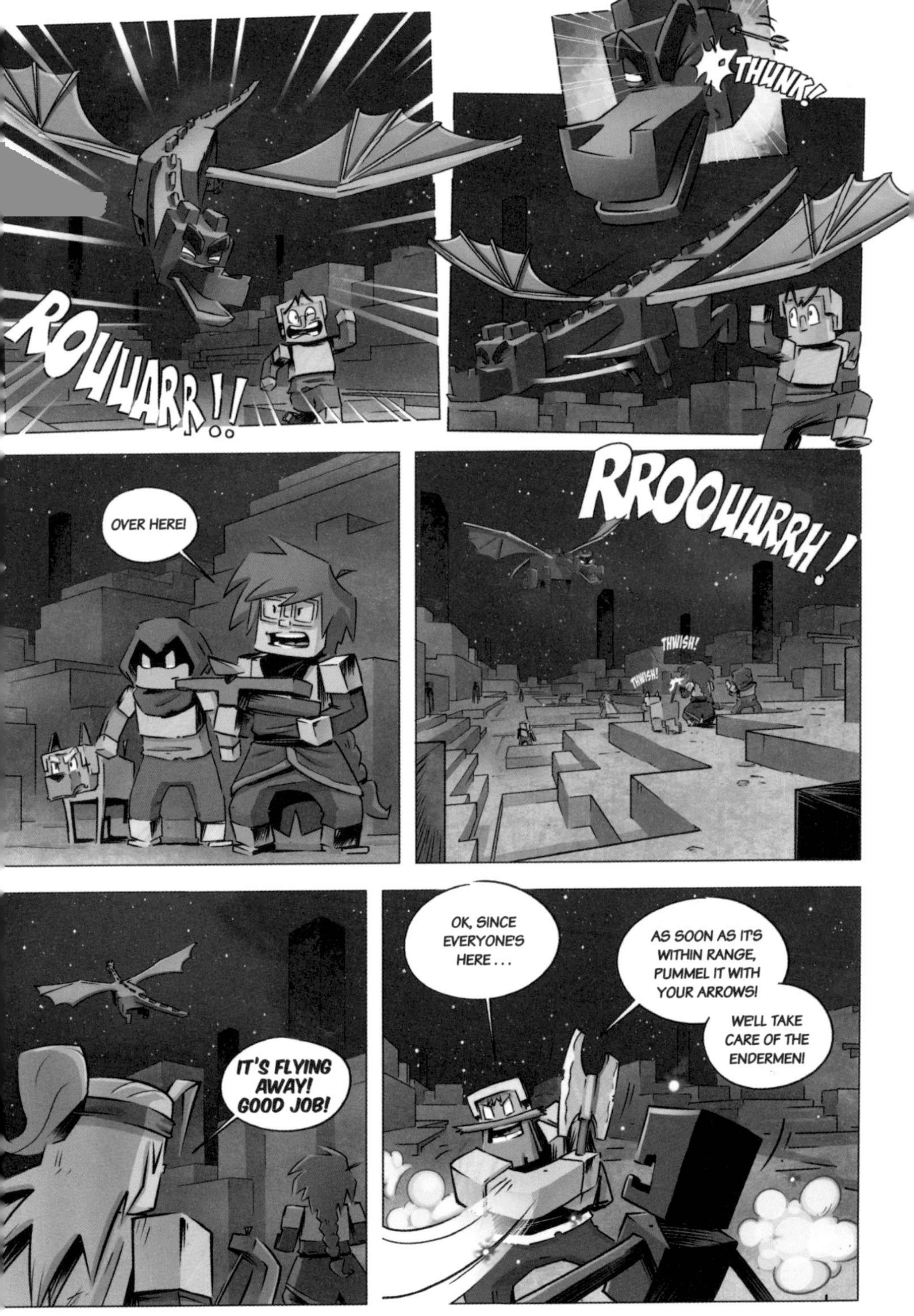
ROUUARR!!
THUNK!
OVER HERE!
RROOUARRH!
THWISH!
THWISH!
IT'S FLYING AWAY! GOOD JOB!
OK, SINCE EVERYONE'S HERE . . .
AS SOON AS IT'S WITHIN RANGE, PUMMEL IT WITH YOUR ARROWS!
WE'LL TAKE CARE OF THE ENDERMEN!

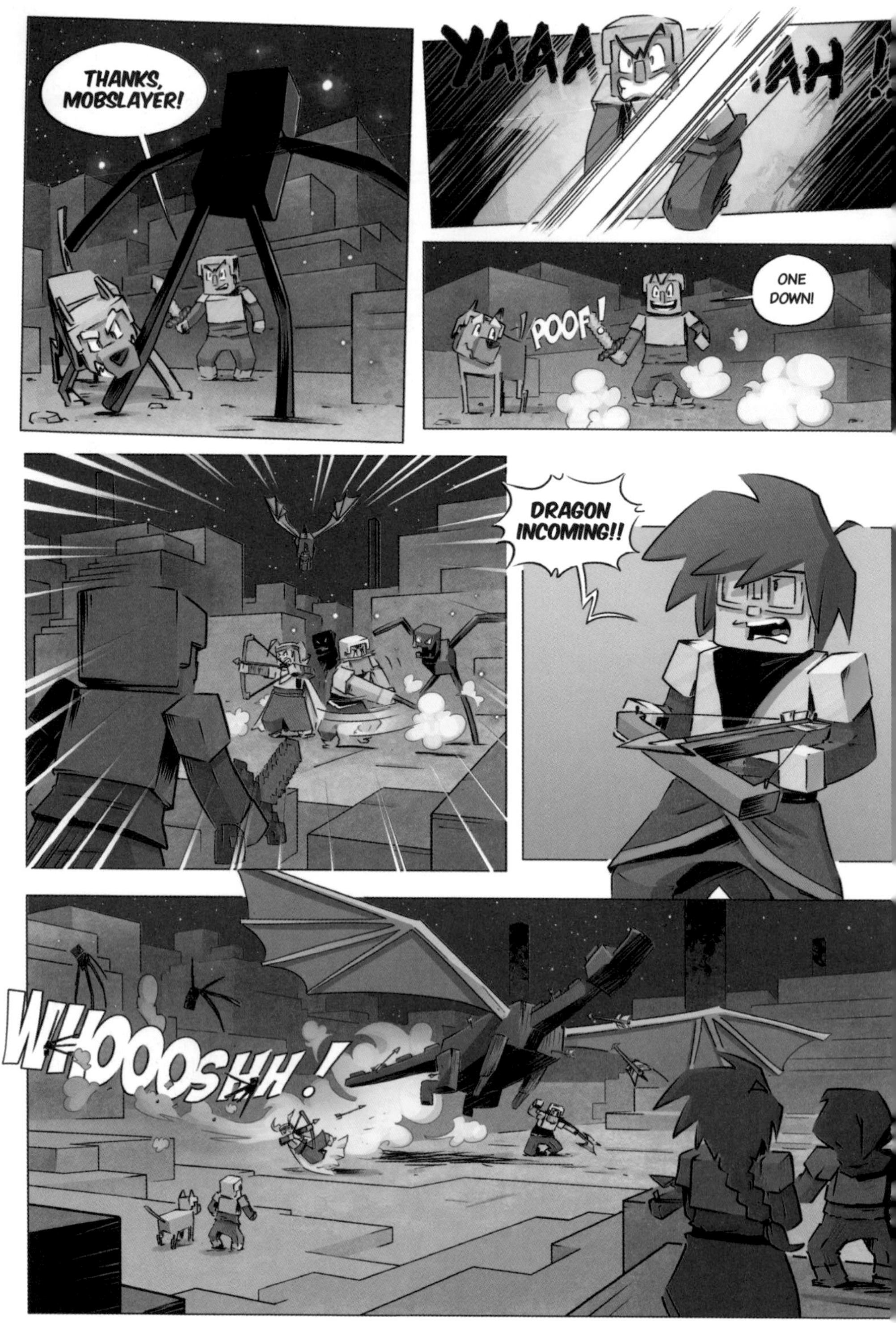
THANKS, MOBSLAYER!
YAAA AH!
POOF!
ONE DOWN!
DRAGON INCOMING!!
WHOOOSHH!

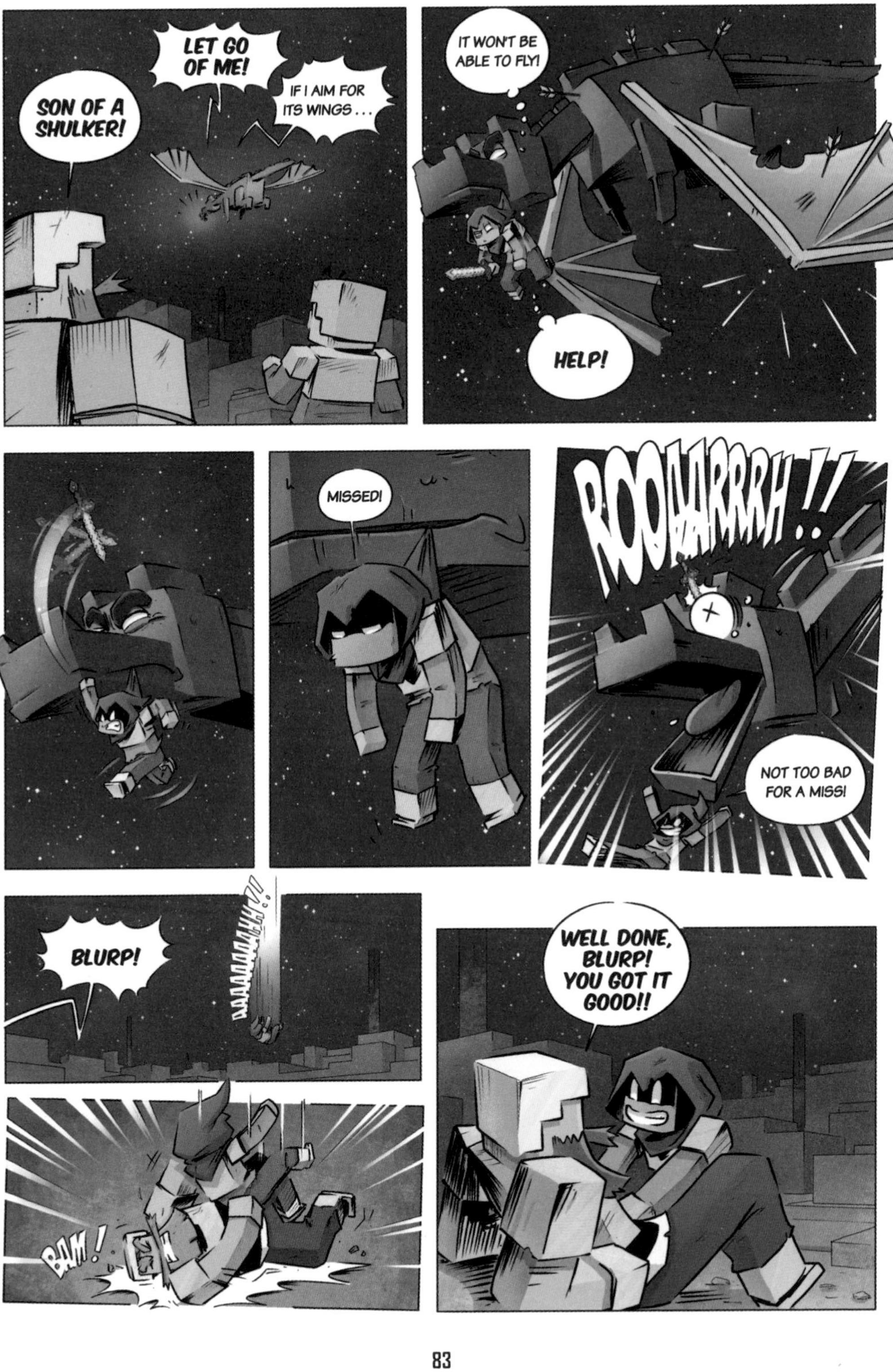
SON OF A SHULKER!
LET GO OF ME!
IF I AIM FOR ITS WINGS . . .
IT WON'T BE ABLE TO FLY!
HELP!
MISSED!
ROOAARRRH!!
NOT TOO BAD FOR A MISS!
BLURP!
BAM!
WELL DONE, BLURP! YOU GOT IT GOOD!!

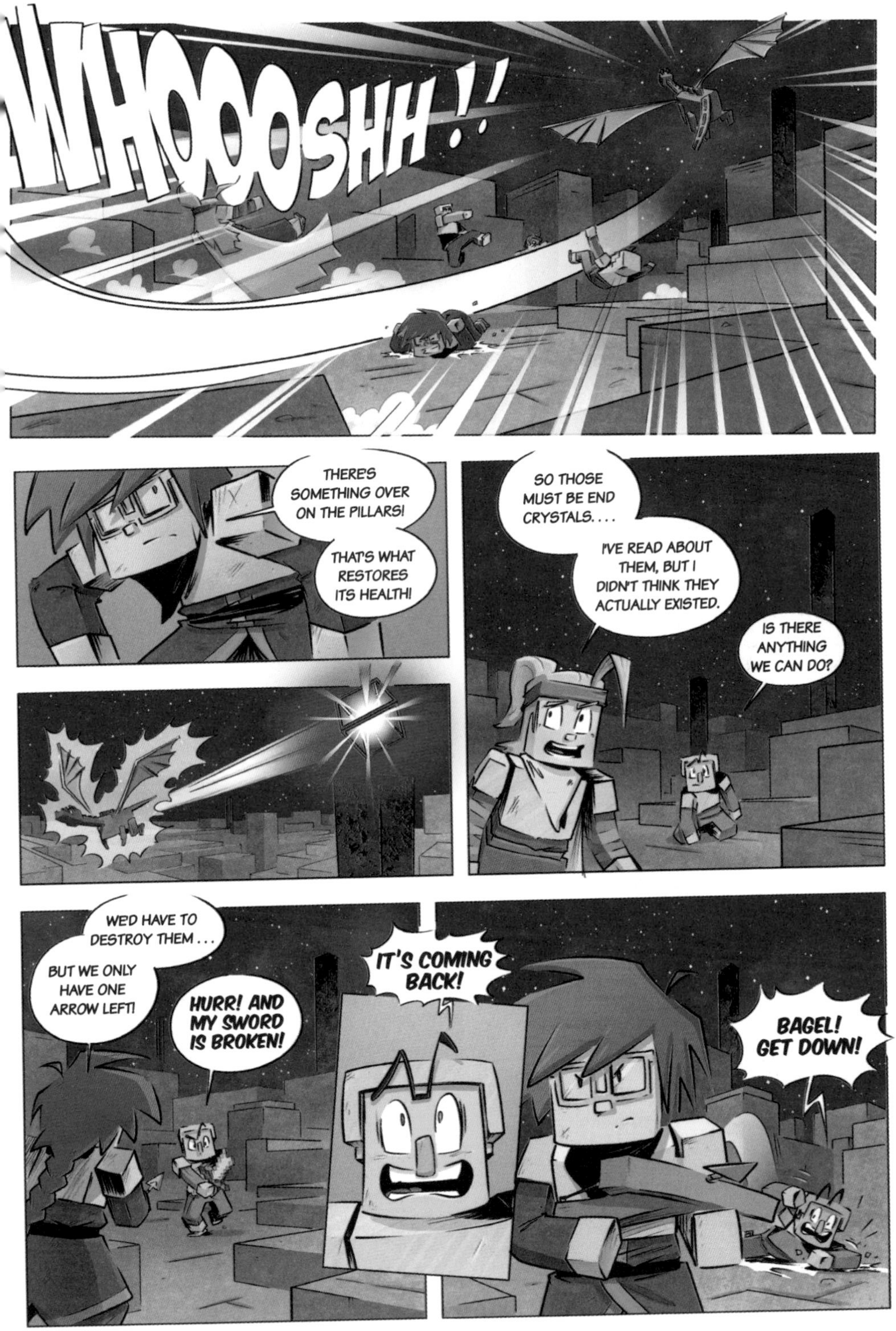
WHOOOSHH!!
THERE'S SOMETHING OVER ON THE PILLARS!
THAT'S WHAT RESTORES ITS HEALTH!
SO THOSE MUST BE END CRYSTALS. . . .
I'VE READ ABOUT THEM, BUT I DIDN'T THINK THEY ACTUALLY EXISTED.
IS THERE ANYTHING WE CAN DO?
WE'D HAVE TO DESTROY THEM . . .
BUT WE ONLY HAVE ONE ARROW LEFT!
HURR! AND MY SWORD IS BROKEN!
IT'S COMING BACK!
BAGEL! GET DOWN!

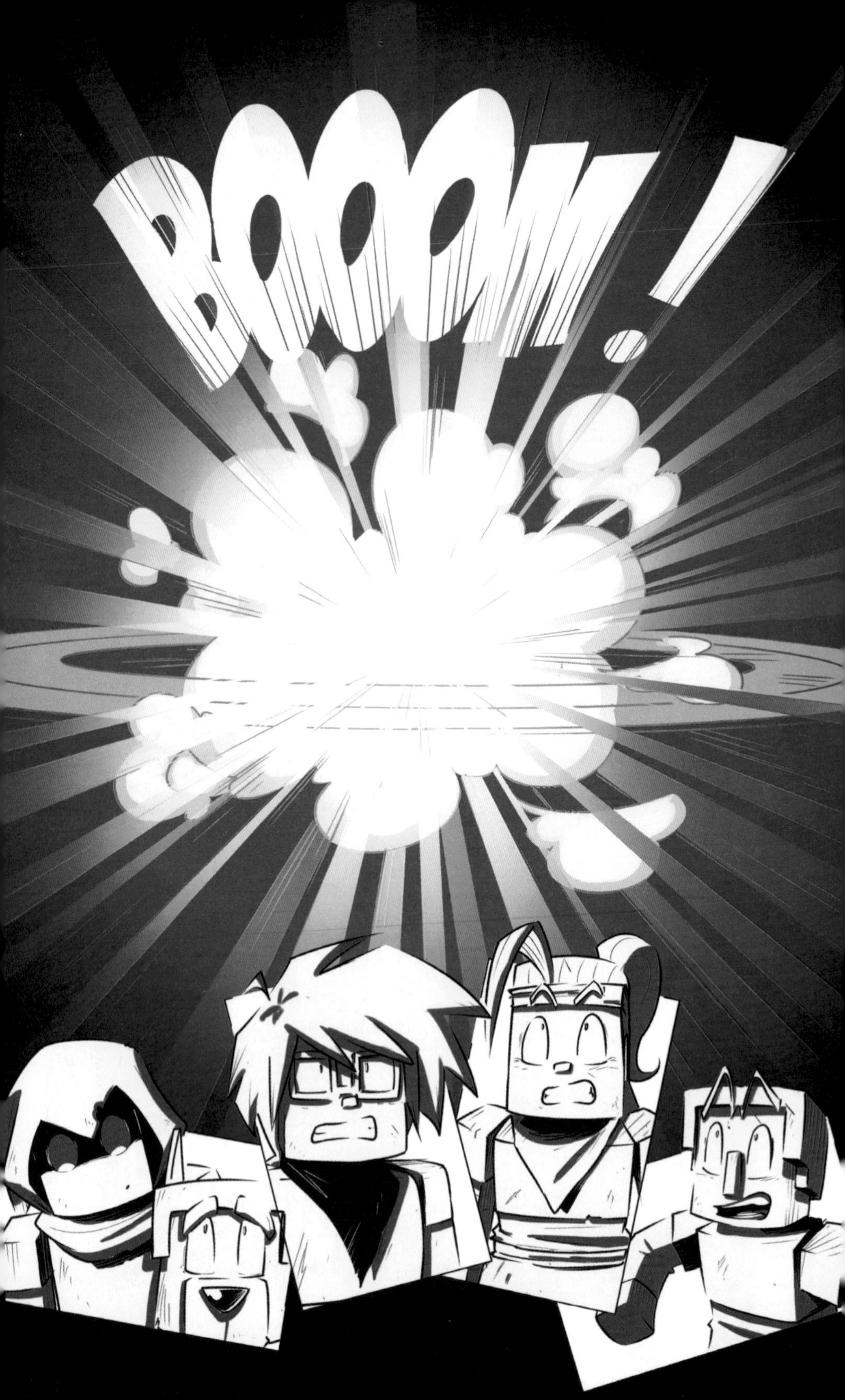
BOOOM!

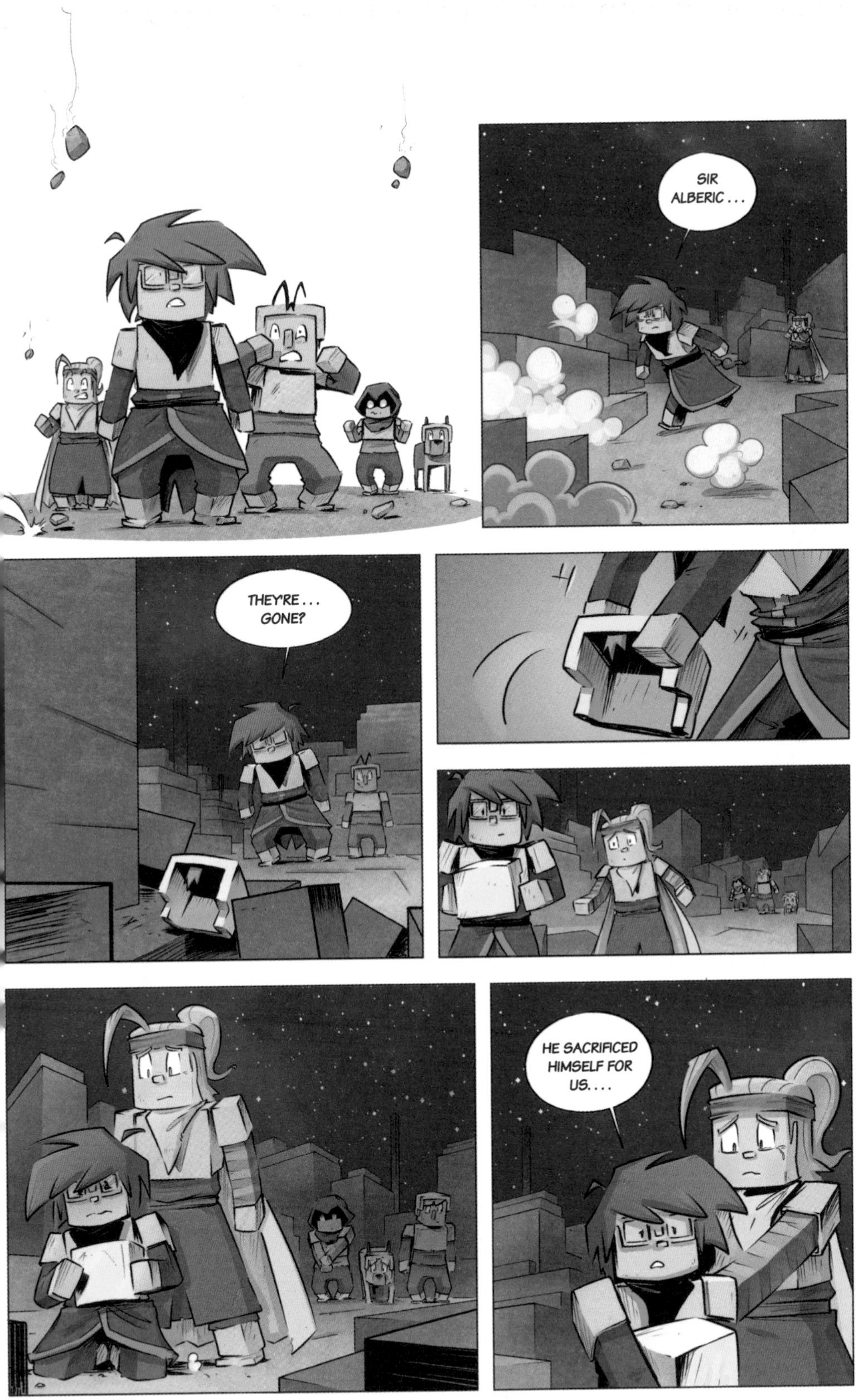

SIR ALBERIC . . .
THEY'RE . . . GONE?
HE SACRIFICED HIMSELF FOR US. . . .

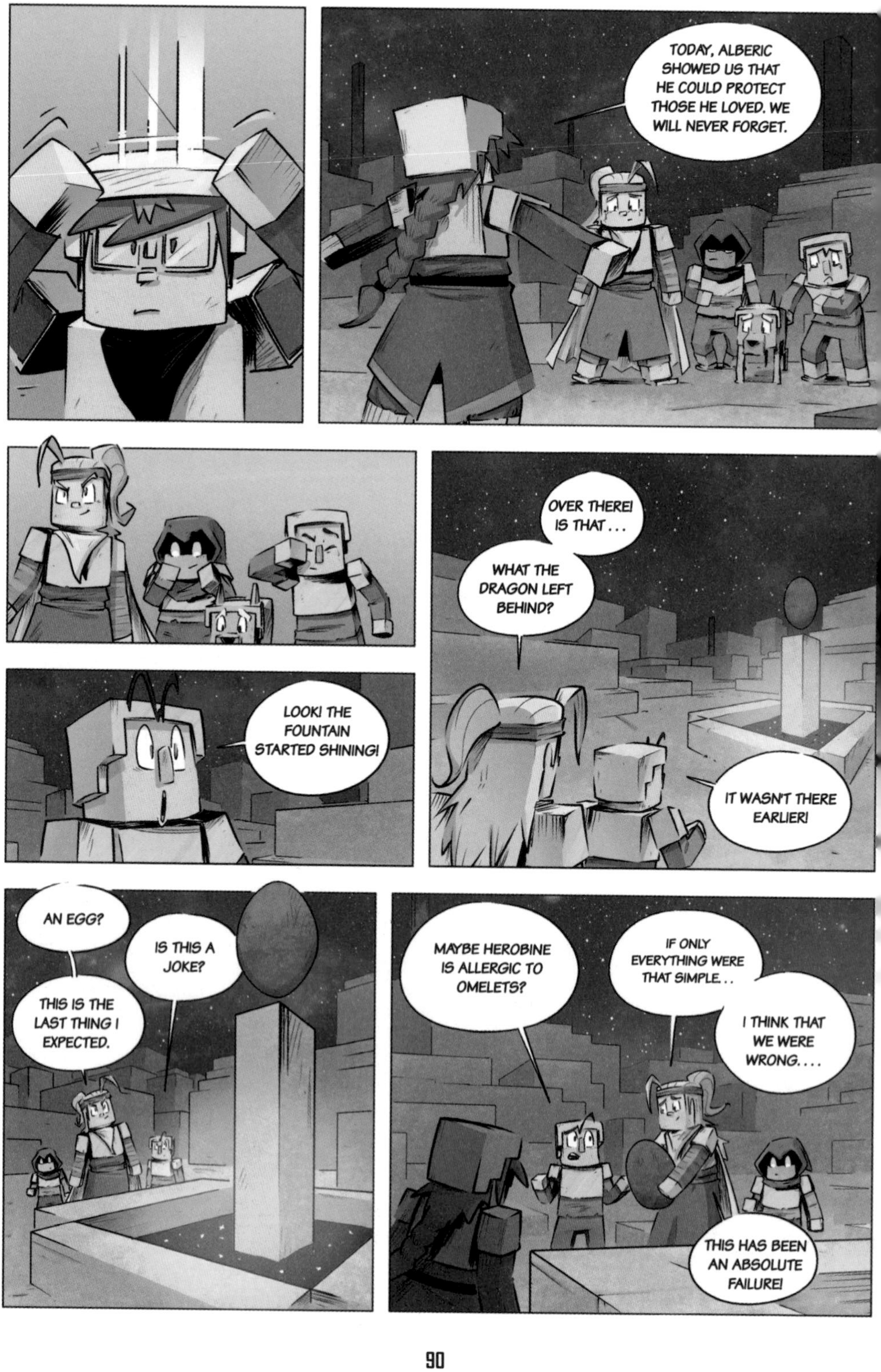
TODAY, ALBERIC SHOWED US THAT HE COULD PROTECT THOSE HE LOVED. WE WILL NEVER FORGET.
LOOK! THE FOUNTAIN STARTED SHINING!
OVER THERE! IS THAT . . .
WHAT THE DRAGON LEFT BEHIND?
IT WASN'T THERE EARLIER!
AN EGG?
IS THIS A JOKE?
THIS IS THE LAST THING I EXPECTED.
MAYBE HEROBINE IS ALLERGIC TO OMELETS?
IF ONLY EVERYTHING WERE THAT SIMPLE. . .
I THINK THAT WE WERE WRONG. . . .
THIS HAS BEEN AN ABSOLUTE FAILURE!

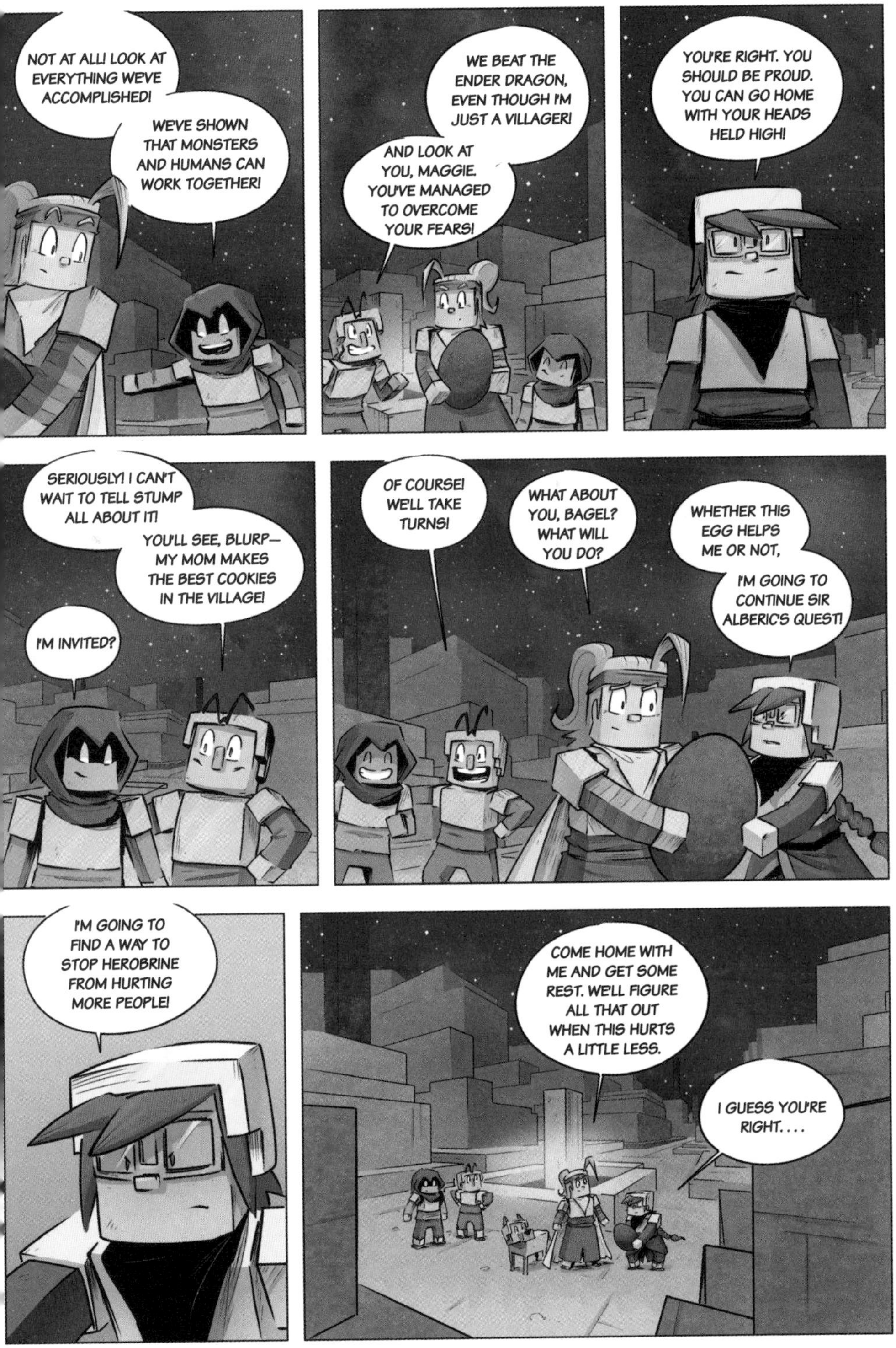
NOT AT ALL! LOOK AT EVERYTHING WE'VE ACCOMPLISHED!
WE'VE SHOWN THAT MONSTERS AND HUMANS CAN WORK TOGETHER!
WE BEAT THE ENDER DRAGON, EVEN THOUGH I'M JUST A VILLAGER!
AND LOOK AT YOU, MAGGIE. YOU'VE MANAGED TO OVERCOME YOUR FEARS!
YOU'RE RIGHT. YOU SHOULD BE PROUD. YOU CAN GO HOME WITH YOUR HEADS HELD HIGH!
SERIOUSLY! I CAN'T WAIT TO TELL STUMP ALL ABOUT IT!
YOU'LL SEE, BLURP— MY MOM MAKES THE BEST COOKIES IN THE VILLAGE!
I'M INVITED?
OF COURSE! WE'LL TAKE TURNS!
WHAT ABOUT YOU, BAGEL? WHAT WILL YOU DO?
WHETHER THIS EGG HELPS ME OR NOT,
I'M GOING TO CONTINUE SIR ALBERIC'S QUEST!
I'M GOING TO FIND A WAY TO STOP HEROBRINE FROM HURTING MORE PEOPLE!
COME HOME WITH ME AND GET SOME REST. WE'LL FIGURE ALL THAT OUT WHEN THIS HURTS A LITTLE LESS.
I GUESS YOU'RE RIGHT. . . .

ABOUT THE AUTHORS

PIRATE SOURCIL is a comic book author known for his blog and his comic series *Le Joueur du grenier*, published by Hugo BD. He is also a fan of geek literature and passionate about the world of gaming.

After studying carpentry, **JEZ** turned to drawing and graphic design and decided to make a career out of it.

ODONE is a French illustrator and specializes in adding color to many comic books.

DIARY OF AN 8-BIT WARRIOR

DIARY OF AN 8-BIT VILLAGER
WARRIOR

Runt, the villager who wants to be a warrior (like Steve)

CUBE KID

AN UNOFFICIAL MINECRAFT ADVENTURE

DIARY OF AN 8-BIT WARRIOR
FROM SEEDS TO SWORDS

The continuing adventures of Runt the villager turned warrior

CUBE KID

AN UNOFFICIAL MINECRAFT ADVENTURE

DIARY OF AN 8-BIT WARRIOR
CRAFTING ALLIANCES

Adventure continues for Runt, the village warrior

CUBE KID

AN UNOFFICIAL MINECRAFT ADVENTURE

DIARY OF AN 8-BIT WARRIOR
PATH OF THE DIAMOND

CUBE KID

AN UNOFFICIAL MINECRAFT ADVENTURE

DIARY OF AN 8-BIT WARRIOR
QUEST MODE

CUBE KID

AN UNOFFICIAL MINECRAFT ADVENTURE

DIARY OF AN 8-BIT WARRIOR
FORGING DESTINY

CUBE KID

AN UNOFFICIAL MINECRAFT ADVENTURE

AND MEET EEEBS, THE MOST NOOBIEST CAT IN THE OVERWORLD!

TALES OF AN 8-BIT KITTEN
LOST IN THE NETHER

Follow the adventures of Eeebs, the noobiest cat in all of Minecraft

CUBE KID

AN UNOFFICIAL MINECRAFT ADVENTURE

TALES OF AN 8-BIT KITTEN
A CALL TO ARMS

See what happens next to Eeebs, the most disobedient cat in all of Minecraft

CUBE KID

AN UNOFFICIAL MINECRAFT ADVENTURE